29 INCHES:

A LONG NARRATIVE POEM

by
mark amerika

chiasmus press
PORTLAND

Chiasmus Press

www.chiasmuspress.com
press@chiasmusmedia.net

PRODUCED AND PRINTED IN THE UNITED STATES OF AMERICA
ISBN: 0-9785499-7-X

cover art: Alex Cahill
The New Radio <http://newradiocomics.com>
cover design: Matthew Warren
layout design: Matthew Warren

One day, I opened up an email which was clearly spam, but what was not clear was why they were sending it to me. They were not trying to sell me anything. The only language inside the body of the email was a random assortment of words that looked to me like a bad William Burroughs cut-up.

But the more I looked at this email, and the others like it that were to follow, the more I began to focus on them and their aesthetic potential. They were much more interesting to read than the glut of supposedly non-spam emails I was receiving on a regular basis from the various bureaucratic institutions I am somehow still tethered to.

This immediately set up a creative challenge for me, one that would test my ability to riff off of these invasive emails in a way that would reposition my relationship with the endless amounts of spam that successfully evaded my spam filter.

The odd language poetry that these emails contained set me off in a direction that I have found helps me deal with spam. Instead of being pissed off by it all, now I USE it as a component in the emotional alchemy I process when writing my fictional verse. Consequently, the new work, entitled *29 Inches*, is an homage to the most hyperbolic email spam I have ever received on the subject of penis enlargement.

In *29 Inches*, irrelevant email becomes relevant source material, a gift from the Spam Gods.

"The measure intervenes, to measure is all we know..."
—WILLIAM CARLOS WILLIAMS, from *Paterson V*

Hi! What are you missing? Click here.
Stop feeling bad about yourself!!
Clueless Is As Clueless Does!
Anus walnut cracking – dig in!
Don't ignore your problems!

Bramble Cork, a fluid stopgap measure
who thinks of himself as a dumpy eel,
relates to his museum art audience a wild story
about an extended night of erotica in Albuquerque
with a girl named Kendall who, after reaching
The Big O
starts spurting volumes
out of nowhere it seems
insisting that she's experiencing a kind of
"horny entropy"
and that it's time for him, Bramble Cork,
to "delouse"!

Where are all these quotes coming from, K-Bomb?
he asks her, using one of the many nicknames
he has for her.

They're just new samples from my recent line
of one-size-fits-all SPAM
for the masses – she whispers
as if sharing a very personal secret with him -
and then pours her head back inside her RIMMjob
sending out another 10,000+ email updates
to her perfectly situated online subscriber base.

The RIMMjob was a personal digital assistant
that was part micro-laptop, part mobile phone,
part wireless email reader, part mp3 player,
and part GPS tracking system.

It was also used as a webcam, a vibrator, and
a stun gun.

The perfect instrument for technomadic spirits
wandering the post-apocalyptic consumer wasteland
of Pax Americana and its VR theme parks.

Being wireless and connected was nothing
if not an opportunity to turn the monetized body
into a fluid entity leaking into the preordained
networked space of flows.

2
4
6
8
10
12
14
16
18
20
22
24
26
28
30
32
34
36
38
40
42
44
46
48
50
52
54

One could easily transport themselves to the
hippy-dippy backwoods Rainbow region of
Colorado's Western Slope, or they could
just as easily hide out in a maple sugar shack
in the make-your-own-jam social libertine
slopes near upstate Vermont.

Hanging with the heavies in Hollywood
playing Mr. Director with the Dreamworks
posse was not out of the question either.

Nor was cribbing in a cheap transient hotel
in The Big Apple living off of nothing but
pinto beans, tofu, brown rice, and endless
tubes of toothpaste.

Presently, they were holed up in what they called
The Mottled Six, a cheap hotel just off I-25
Between Albuquerque and Taos.

When Bram turned back to his own RIMMjob,
Kendall snuck in a shopping digression.

Surfing the electronautical bay of consumer peegs,
she cast a circumnavigational eye in Bram's
easily targeted direction and then, upon further
clickitude, found herself on the website
for the Fashionably Yours Network.

Aren't these colors terrif, asks Kendall
pointing at a large jpeg of a camouflage
camisole: dark brown, oatmeal and beige
with one deep earthy pocket.

Kerouac wore khakis (she says)
it's true (a bit smarmy and superior)
but today's ideal poetess is more inclined
to go with the Diesel-Aldo-Versace
Mesopotamia line of measure.

Of course (she went on - in a nod
to her ineluctable beatitude), the contemporary

poetess dressed in full-blown *camo* khakis
while owing a hidden debt to the insanely
out of their heads Italiano Futurists
will inevitably catch a sacred glimpse into
the ecstatic mystical visions of the prototypically
ex-urban real. In this regard (she cocks her
head at 40 degree angle with her tongue
only slightly lulling on the edge of her lower lip)
she will always and forever drive her Lamborghini
to Aspen to BUY these *new italic hybrids*
in second-hand consignment shops. She
is a poetess, after all, and trust funds only
go so far.

Second thread, best thread, Bramble teases –
but she interrupts him and continues her
color commentary while surfing
the online catalogue -

For we are all (she says in mock dramatic tones)
always and already ON consignment, deferring
our ultimate hook-up with Mr. Destiny who, by the way,
looks perpetually disheveled and overstressed
from having to account for all of his
passed on angels of mercy and their
ever quickening multitudes.

Bram feels apocryphal, feels some more, feels
again, then comes out with it: "is that some kind of
trendy bohemian camouflage outfit? Trying
to attract the NASCAR Dads to your porn site?"

Nope (she insists) just Cammywear.
Rugged outdoorsy hipsterwear
for the glam webcam *girl on the go.*

Clothing is your first line of defense
(she says this wistfully, like she wants
to believe it). If home is where the heart
is, then Homeland Security begins with
the body: our last frontier...

...before the invasive forces of technocapitalism
use their nanotechnological superiority to calmly
enter your bloodstream under the illusion of
protecting your borders (says Brammy, throwing out
his Popeye arm and turning his palm outward like a hail to
the coming furor).

Kendall herself recently reached number three
on the list of most-watched amateur porn
webcam sites where her *oeuvre*, her simultaneous
and continuous fusion of online performance art,
simply entitled

Superfuckalicious.Com

was moving up the charts faster than her
outlaw spam could even begin to take credit for.

Or maybe what I mean is Tammywear,
(she says, trying to get back on subject)
wiretapping her consumer subconscious
so that she can *read her own mind* as it
drifts into the fashionable hereafter.

Tammy? (asks Bram, knowing full well
whom she is referring to)

Yes, Tammy (she says) -
You heard of Tommy, the Hilfilger
Pilferer? This is one Tammy Verb,
my old sorority sister from my undergraduate
years back in Buddhist Amerika!

She always referred to her birthplace and
college home town, Boulder, Colorado,
as "Buddhist Amerika!"

(always punctuating her acknowledgment with
a spunkily-charged exclamation point!)

She shows him a picture of lithe blond perkiness
full of Colgate smiles
dressed in camo.

Looking in K's RIMMjob
Bramble recognized the woman in the digital pic
as an embedded reporter in Iraq who somehow
always puts a pleasant spin on the ensuing media carnage.

Tammy versus Tommy? I'll take the camo-sheathed
shiksa any day of the week! (confirmed Bram)

Bram's RIMMjob plays an electronic drone loop
suggesting there may be new source material
clogging up his networked arteries.

He sees it's a new spam message and cuts it up
for her ears only, a kind of spontaneous bop poetics
dressed in dot.com newspeak that he himself has
become totally absorbed with:

> "Can the use-value of that special little man whose
> intrepid impersonation of the millionaire next door
> perform open heart surgery on you, implementing
> mounds of melting chocolate machetes reworking
> your emotional architecture in a vain attempt to
> help you move beyond that perpetually poignant yet
> puzzled look of pampered indifference masquerading
> as total contempt? What's so natural about becoming
> so bodily modified and urbanely outfitted that you
> successfully conceal yourself in the non-native
> environment? And is it a calumny of retail politics
> that you can now get the same exact camisole on ebay
> for half the price?"

Seeing nor hearing nary a response from K,
B ends his hard bop drama on a conciliatory note:

> "I wanna be your PayPal. I pay, you pal.
> You play, I pale, in comparison. Without
> You, I impale my heart -- with pall."

It all sounds a bit too pell-mell to me,
K pretends to not decode, and then she shoves
    her white-socked foot
up his hanging endnote saying

"Brammy, it's time to delouse!"

at which point she lets out this Wicked Witch
of the West cackle full of laughing death, as if it were all
somehow bottled up inside her, a vintage death,
1945, Auschwitz - or was it just some more of that
fine Rhein whine?

Her parents were from Germany, Professors who
took positions at the big state research university
although she herself was born in and TOTALLY American.

She said it again, though somewhat creepier as if to
get on his nerves would somehow help structurally
reintegrate his spinal chord and force him
to use more backbone
while evolving his interiorized 3-D narrative patterning:

"Brammy, it's time to delouse!"

But he'll have absolutely none of that, and uncorks
another set of spam-generated Q's for her perfectly engendered A:

"Where do we find ourselves? Caught struggling for
breath in between a series of interventionist spam
messages of which we still do not know the poetic
extremes? Does our deep animal sleep linger like
a tranced-out mesh of all things swimming with
glitter? Who are the ghostlike apparitions of memory
enhancement that glide through these exceptional
foreign languages languidly lapping their tongues at
the tasteless fucks that mutilate our common sense
of the real? Are we destined to become ephemeral
lovers on the lower end of the stream where the
putrescent stains of the industrial coronations have
leaked their morbid fluid? And why do we have to
work so hard for a debt we'll never acquit? So that
we may have the privilege to download a banal
orgy of Total Information Awareness at x frames per
second? Does that make us voyeuristic busy bodies
or just idle thrill seekers menacing our minds with
perpetual sideshows of fear-drenched anxiety and

the promise of pornographic Armageddon?! And
what of this endless, dysfunctional war? Is that why
amateur porn sites are the new stars of the revitalized
net economy? Was that another multi-culti boytoy at
the end of your long dog leash or was it just the latest
dark victim of your radical separatist neoconservative
butcher scheme? What opium waters are pouring
down our throats, bloating our eyeballs, infesting our
guts, and circulating inside our paranormal psyche?!
Do we just prefer to submit? Does it send a wicked
sense of unrelenting excitement through our always
overexposed plenty-proud pores of portal logic?
Where is the evanescent lubricity of superfuckalicious
sentience when you need it?!"

But Kendall had no A's for him this time,
as she had already planted her head deep
back into the undertow of her own tangerine RIMMjob
drowning in the mp3 world contained inside
her furry green headphones, from The Gap.

Tired Of Losing Trades?
Cheating Wives!
68% of women are unsatisfied
BUY FAT BLAST NOW!
feel the vitality! Algebraic
Seeking the Man or Woman of your dreams?
Let It Be Me

Mobility's the rule
and Bramble shifts his vermin body
over to the other side of the bed
repositions the live web cam
so that it now angles in from
a higher location on top
of the bed board
where it looks straight into the face
of the now attentive K

He slides off
the bed's edge
stands on his feet
and tries to elevate the conversation
into a different subsection of his
spam-infused hemorrhaging cerebellum
pulling three random words from the string
of blather that was now ticking across
the push media screen of his lubricated
RIMMjob apparatus.

Let's call it the *Romeo Sinai Ticket*,
he said.

The what? (Kendall)

The Romeo Sinai Ticket.

Think of lover, he says,
think of me, Bram Corkle,
a romance language peppered
with the excesses of a cyberpidgin
mucking about in his stylized sty.

I'm your dog (he said) (point blank).

But I thought you were a specie-ist,
an anti-pet proponent of wildlife for
All (she insisted).

Nope, Cork volleyed, I never said that.
It's close, but I am totally FOR animals.
ALL ANIMALS. They are you as you
are me and we are all together.

Riiiiight, she countered: see how they run
like peegs from a gun, see how they fry.

Think of me as a human veterinarian (he went on)
which is oxymoronic and disproves the obvious point,
but let's steer clear of what we think is obvious
and insist that if most humans are robots, and robots
are cured of disease through nanotechnological

programming that rewrites the inner body code,
then as a human veterinarian I would focus
on non-robot humans who need special care,
like rubbing, or licking, or eating out.

But tell me Romeo, how would you discern
the robots from the non-robot humans?

The way I always have, through my animal magnetism,
and besides (he bent toward her with
a slow wink that promised an endless forever)
I am often known to have a taste for vegans,
and all vegans are non-robotic human beans.

Le Gumans (she interjected – but he went on)

    Consequently
(Cork said this as he slid his sly eye
down toward the gleaming flesh
of her approximate Other)
my attraction to You.

Well it sure beats meat! (she said)
jerking her whole body up while
mimicking a joe-blow wank off.

I like the way you do that with your hand,
said Bram. Even when mocking the onanist
Holymen, you still seem to maintain a respectful
attitude toward gentleness and delicate palming.

Well (she said) that's because when I think of wank,
I think of You (and mocked his sly wink).

Well, thank you too, K-Y Jelly!

She hated it when he called her K-Y Jelly.
She preferred something more queenly, like
Royal Jelly. Or one her other faves, Jelly Katt.

But the Bram kept rambling, speaking in spam tongue, saying
things like "Any given romeo clocks in chicks. Looking
for quick sinai relief? Take the ma huang fix. Feel the wet

circumference of superfuckalicious sentience as it becomes
a juicy tangerine dream. Lick the RIMMjob then slip into
something more comfortable, like surface memory dancing."

Nixxxx that one, screeched K, that is not allowable. As the
gross webcam spam monger par excellence, with a sizeable
bank account to prove it, I can tell you, the superfuckalicious
sentient machine rarely becomes a wet and juicy tangerine
dream. Unless I have King Dolphin at the ready, and for that
– I need TIME.

King Dolphin was her vibrating mammal cousin
who with the flick of a switch, would nurture
into being a thousand and one plateaus lost
in the fog of night.

Whenever she was super horny,
her skin flaking toward entropy –
she'd turn on Dolphy and let the transmissions begin.

And when did you first realize that
I was becoming a vegan? (she asks)
I mean, I just started and have yet
to seriously bring it up with you.

I could tell by the way you just ate me,
(he said, without second thought). You
were very chic, slow chewing, like
a cat on mescaline.

A Royal Tigress licking my mortal wounds.

And this Romeo Sinai Ticket?

Oh that, yes, I was hoping you would forget.
Yep, (he was looking for some self-assurance)
think of a lover. Think of me, the barding bramble
who only awaits your secret death pact for ultimate
conclusions .   .   .
Think of me as a
young, dumb, and full of cummmmmmmmmmmm
blazing Sinai mountain burning with Alpha Omega intensity,
stirred by the majestic coming

of the Thick,
glorious in cocky bent.

Sounds like Thick tricksterism, the lovely
Ms. K responded. Is this the new crude
romanticism? The one filtered through
the best reality TV minds of our generation
destroyed by Ritilin and suffering from epiphanies
of color coded fear mongering who prancing around
in their second-hand designer underwear listen
to the Terror blaring from their dot.bombed psyches?

Ah, but ain't that the Ticket
(he asked her, moving in close)
ain't that where You come in?

She too got off the bed now
and they were standing at opposite ends
separated by a queensize spermstained mattress
in the Mottled Six.

He adjusted the webcam so that it became
a wide lens taking in only the bed while
picking up their muted dialogue:

Bramble Cork (she said) it's time to degummify you!

But why? (he asked) I'm happy to stretch the truth,
especially in the name of Ur-Reality and other
variegated forms of fiction. Besides, I've known
it to get closer to the Truth than any absolute
version thereof.

Because (she said) those always ON
consignment must have a ready set go
array of contingency plans. Contingent
truths mark one with the efficacious
results of a truly lived experience.

The improvisational life, he murmured,
but she was in a kind of trance already
blasting past him:

And besides (it was if her aura were in countdown)
only the connotative accede to
the congestive benediction of leaky burrows.

Sounds like you're dropping
into spam mode (he cautioned her)

"Quiet," she said, "the noisy smart glove is thinking."

Oh no, he said, and now with quotes!

"Shhhh." (said K) "The green sofa remembers
and the eight calloused hands calm down and
still their smart round car is angry."

No! You must stop! It's like Gertrude Stein
is trying to sell me drugs from Canada!

"No waiting rooms," she riffed on his allusion,
"overnight shipping, secret packaging, and fully confidential.
Only overnight and fully confidential and waiting. Only
the waiting and a fully confidential prescription
with no embarrassment. With embarrassment there is depression,
with depression there is revulsion, and with revulsion
there is the shipping of secrecy. The shipping of secrecy."

You MUST stop (he pleaded).

"Must?" asked K, "must as in must her hairy
binoculars snore while her brothers secretly erase
sofa memory? Forget these embarrassing smells that the
car backseat walks all over my softest of memories with?
Only an illusory blowfish suffering from the revulsion
of an aforementioned new and crude romanticism, would think
something like that. What happened to Romeo signing
off his tickets to Oblivion from high atop the summit
of his hemp-headed Mountain? Did he finally implode?

Let me count the ways."

And to the bathroom she went.

Bram was falling into what he once dubbed
efflorescent skullduggery.

The Ticket That Imploded.

CAN YOU DIG IT he yelled at the cosmos?

CAN – YOU – FUCKING – DIG IT?

How long would she be in there?

1
3
5
7
9
11
13
15
17
19
21
23
25
27
29
31
33
35
37
39
41
43
45
47
49
51
53

> *Take Once, Last all Weekend!*
> *Feeel Yooooounger Todaay*
> *Keeep heeer cuuummiiing all niiiiiight*
> *increase your penis size by 29 inches*
> *i knoooow your noot scaaaaared to try*
> *Amaaaaaazing Lubriiiiiiicaaaaaaation*
> *No need to cross the border...*

Free delivery...

Check this out my lil chickadee

[Bram was experiencing

host closed connection

in realtime]

I've got a portable kitchen
with hot plate, pots and pans
and all the survivalist technology
one needs to Eat A Horse!

[and as he unpacked their camping gear

from his humongous backpack,

he went on the offensive]

But being that you are a tasty
vegan whose Florentine body
skins my suggestiveness
with panting breaths of carbon
dioxide, I will remain loyal
to your anti-carnivoracious predilections!

Anything for you twinkle toes!

So open the door and come out of there
or else I'm coming in after you!

No reaction. Not even a freshly red
painted twinkle toe
peep nor scratch.

Listen honeybun, the bees may not be
vegan, but their ceremonial love juice
is just as sweet and sticky as that
bluish sexual tint you just swallowed
out of me a mere 30 minutes ago, and
I have smeared some luscious Royal Jelly
on a graham cracker just for you!

Come out my little kumquat, come out
and give your good Uncle Cork a rich
slavering of that precious amber cream
that pours out of your pores!

I'll reposition all of the microwebcams and flatter
this disgusting space with the depth
and breadth of our wireless configuration
and then we can continue streaming
our prototypical hyperheterosexual
commie liberal conspiracy
of nothing but the drip and swine
of our raw bodies spilling

a potent and formerly forbidden
set of mores only WE have the power
to distribute to our peer to peer network
unfolding in the swollen pornosphere!

Besides, as far as mores go, I say mores smores!
Come on out my little kumquat, come out
and give your Uncle Cork the pleasure
of your cracklin' rice krispies!

Still there was nothing but silence,
or what the spam marketers foolishly
refer to as *militant touchiness.*

Cork tried a different tact, this time
making it clear that he was not going
to talk to a door all night, and that
she needed to start thinking about the
restless Others scattered throughout the world
all of them personally responsible for
"deepening your pockets" and who she needed
to reconnect with asap - the nomadic webcam
of indifference was blinking red and her
hungry masses were impatiently waiting for
the green light so they could reestablish
a connection with all of her
every bit of her
her virtual her
the hertual
verb. . .

To come!

He yelled it again:

> *To come!*

> *It's in your unwritten contract!*

He knew that would get her. Her guilt trip
was way beyond the norm when she stopped to think
about it. For she, the self-manufactured K-doll,

was the ultimate in entrepreneurial reputation,
the heavenly hoagie of the spam generation
finding endless nuance of language and sales-pitch
and pristinely positioned bodily screenshots,
metaphorical button-pushing, virtual love
offerings, not to mention her daily blog entries
with all of her preferences listed so as to make it all too clear
that she was unquestionably the perfect mate
for any hip wannabe bohemian workaholic
looking for a smart sexy chick who was categorically
saying Fuck You to the immoral majorities
and their jesusfuckingchrist mocking of ethics
and corruption - like the guy running for Senator
who was quoted as saying that he favored the death
penalty for any abortion clinic doctor who stole away a
fetus' life. . . *what a total dipshit!*

What idiocy! She would inject her own brand name
doggy-style nomadicism over the net just to
ridicule his ridiculous ass as if to say to
puritanically crazy America and its rotting
mind of chemically induced fundamentalist pollution

   can't touch this!

What about our audience, for christ-fucking-sakes,
(he screamed at the door) - for she was *his* bread and butter too,
and she knew it.

But she didn't say a word or make a sound. She was the
master of her own domain (superfuckilicious.com) and
called all the shots. She was the Boss Mistress and nobody,
not even Bram, was going to control her very next move. She
was an independent woman for crying out loud! You don't
go to Andover Brown (B.A) Yale (M.F.A.) and the Whitney
Independent Study Program to become an anarchic aerobics
teacher reaching new cardiovascular heights deep in the
heart of Buddhist Amerika!

Not that she had not tried that too, everything
from spinning to body sculpture to pilates to
Transhistorical Yoga, not to mention a series of affairs
with pumped up Fitballs moaning and groaning

in various positions all to the tune of Supertramp
and the artist formerly known as Prince
until one day she opened up her then unfiltered IN box
and saw a string of subject headings that went

Immediately Catch the attention of Women
Sex dates are simple and real
Sing.le woman looking for someone to love
Oral Hygiene Match: Someone For You
Hey my name is Cindy

and something clicked.

It was a kind of spontaneous reeducation -
a translucent body-brain achievement
not just a light bulb going off in her head
but a rhizomatic spread of hotwired intuition
sending scintillating buzzcups of eureka enthusiasm
throughout her Central Nervous System.

What was made clear and precisely too obvious
to the point where she wondered where she had been
and what it was that had locked her in such stoic
self misapprehension, was that she could become
Anything - Everything - Anyone she wanted to become -
and that she could transfluctuate her mounting morbidity -
her overly contextualized set of personalized complications -
into a fluid stream of highly contagious media viruses
and simply start role-playing the excessive Others
she had always dreamt of, poetically
but that had now become a cluster of hungry digital personas
nestling deep within her ever-expanding psychosphere -
an evolving Republic of easily manipulated phantom beings
filling the void
inside the networked space of flows.

These randomly generated and hyperlinked verbal
Othernesses, who in the real world of physical thereness
were needlessly tripped up by having to be in a certain

place in the here and now, were free to roam the vast
electrosphere, and could radically quickchange themselves
into a sexy mélange of luscious freethinking digital beings
promenading their sleek aesthetic fitness to those who
were absolutely turned on by such blatant adulteration
dropping all pretension while systematically
losing their virginity
in the cyberpsychogeography of A Sexy Schizopolis -
an architectonic You-topia made of pixels and flesh
whose enervating scaffolding was stripped
to the raw bone of naked self-desire
while wholeheartedly playing right into
the logic of specto-situationist technocapitalism   .   .   .

In other words

She was free to be whatever she wanted to be
and being the sole or maybe soul proprietor
of superfuckalicious.com playing out her
overly excitable exhibitionist streak
was exactly what she was put on this good Earth for.

She knew she had the body
the temperament, the ego
the belly of necessity
to share her image with
        the connected .   her
            constructed image .   .

        always aware of
                where it   wanted
                        to   go
                                    next .   .

This was what it meant to be totally liberated!
To blow her boyfriend LIVE
on her own terms
in front of thousands of tuned in subscribers
and to do it for more than the money

            [what was money anyway?
            a cheap excuse for living
            in the coin of the realm -

and besides, if living well
was the best revenge, then
she was a revengeful bitch
in spades, because she was
way beyond living well, she
was what they call *living proof!*]

      Her
proof of concept did not need the backing
of angel investors or Yahoo or ebay or iFuck -

no, all she needed was the Goo-goo-googling eyes
of zillions upon zillions of Goddess worshippers
and the guerilla marketing tactics of uncontrollable
word-of-mouse!

And out of this selfgenerated monster meme

      Superfuckilicious.com

would emerge a niche, a
porno niche – something she had slowly
evolved on her own, with Bram, her ace
in the hole.

She knew she had the body
the brains, the apparatus
consciousness, to share her image
    to share her image with
    the connected . .

And the connected were her perfect
demographic: computer-savvy, sex
starved, well-to-do boys and girls
who, uncertain about their own sexual
identities or worse, too sure of it
for their own good, would pay top dollar
just to have an occasional peek inside
the leaky pink zones of the raging K-girl!

Although her online moniker was, of course,
like her online identity, quite separate from

1
3
5
7
9
11
13
15
17
19
21
23
25
27
29
31
33
35
37
39
41
43
45
47
49
51
53
55
57
59
61
63
65
67
69
71
73
75
77
79

her given family name – though not her
family values!

[what were family values anyway?
an Orwellian buzzterm for the Totally Lost
robotic brethren burning in the TV kiln -
and besides, if family values were
truly all they were cracked up to be,
then why did she feel that her
womb of internal necessity, Her Motherly
Earthness, was what drove her to reach out
and share her blood-erect verbs with all of these
overzealous others?!]

Online, she was Felicia Catt, and instead
of the tall, voluptuous, athletically well-built blond
all of her friends knew her to be, she was a tall,
voluptuous, athletically well-built raven-haired
beauty who wore a variety of jet-black wigs
and who – as her preferences page wickedly pointed out –
liked best to take it from behind, to lift
her ass up high toward the heavens so that her man,
in this case, the raving stark mad poet Bramble Cork,
could set his rockhard rig deep up inside her,
reaching magic G-spots never before encountered,
both soft g's and hard g's – even silent g's – all of them
magically pulsating with the zesty zeroing in of

the "hook-up" zeitgeist.

That feeling, that feeling of getting up
high and deep inside and touching spots
never reached before, almost wondering if
there were, in fact, a third intestine or,
if not that, a third sex organ facetiously
put up the ovary tract to mimic the depths
of the intestinal tract itself . . .

as if babyshit and shitting babies were now
one and the same thing and wouldn't getting
pregnant just ruin the whole thing!

(she wondered / he dreaded

      but why bring it up?)

   . . .

Queen Bee of the Amateur Porn Universe
Felicia Catt at superfuckilcious.com
was perfectly situated in her rightful domain.

Breaking into the marketplace of ideas
was one way of looking at it.

Uncapping the honeycomb structure
of her post-waste case mind
was another.

But why was she hiding in the bathroom
inside the sleazy Mottled Six?

I'm coming in after you, Kendall!

But the door was locked and Bramble
took a gamble
pulled out his infamous bloody valentine
got lucky
and jigged the lock open.

The door flew open as if porting him
to a floating theater of the mind where
the only option was to perpetually *drift*
in the digital afterlife, a space
that never returned a gaze and wanted
very much to absorb his entire persona.

It was if he were suddenly thrust into the
giant pupil of outer space, seeing nothing but
black, being nothing but black, surrounded
by nothing but a huge black hole which he was
sure he had entered except now, belatedly,
he realized that the huge black hole of his existence
was actually capable of leaking information

2
4
6
8
10
12
14
16
18
20
22
24
26
28
30
32
34
36
38
40
42
44
46
48
50
52
54
56
58
60
62
64
66
68
70
72
74
76
78
80

(what a revelation!) – and the information
it leaked was evil, for it revealed how old
he was and how old he would ever be, and
this was information he would have preferred
to remain kept inside some secret dark place
on the outskirts of human knowledge.

He immediately saw that she was gone,
the levity of the situation pronounced
as the bathroom had no roof and the sky
was full of cumulus kelp.

An underworld illusion of water and sky
lost in the false pretense of discovering
a new solar system whose sun had finally burnt out,
his silky dream technology of conscious flow
was rhythmically carrying his connected Otherness
up into the heavens, deep into the sea –
        simultaneously -
and Bramble felt like an inside-out
upside-down Man.

        Where could she have disappeared to?

She had taken her tangerine RIMMjob and
a back-up microwebcam into the bathroom
with her so she could easily and without a thought
continue streaming her adulterated media
content over the wireless networks.

        But without him? Her ace-in-the-hole?

That microwebcam, which they affectionately
called Nosy, had been inserted into every
possible orifice and from every possible
angle of every possible interior and exterior
location used for their moveable fuckfeast
as they nomadically wandered the spacey desert
of the collective unconscious they called their home.

One time, Nosy was placed deep inside
the anal walnut crack of Catt's oozing bunghole

and the ensuing theater of cruelty created
quite the brouhaha over the Net. Now known
as the infamous Runny Shit Fuck with
close-ups of Bram's logocentric tool
pummeling away while further forcing the issue,
the number of new subscriptions almost doubled
in a day, giving more credence to the theory
that Reality TV is still a viable form of
consumer edutainment and that streaming
docudramas posing as amateur avant-porn
is not only the wave of the future, but
the D-I-Y certitude of the Now!

Forget ebooks, these were leaking she-books!

Felicia herself was eager to write the obligatory blog entry in her immediate follow-up to the runny slam dance she and Bram performed for her well-trained monkey masses.

In the blog, she wrote:

> Sometimes you have to take care of an itch. If I get a mosquito bite on my leg or on my neck, I feel I just *have* to scratch it and let it know I'm there! I have no hard feelings for the mosquito. After all, who wouldn"t want to take a crack at playing vampire to my willing flesh. Mr. Mosquito is a pirate lover who sucks the blood out of my waiting body, one small injection at a time, and I only wish he could suck me some more, to make me dizzy with hallucinations of what I perceive to be the unreal. Because without the unreal, there is no real. And I live for the real.
>
> But what about when you get an itch deep inside you? Up into those dark places where you regularly decompose yourself as a body artist? What about those creepy caves of solid waste management where who you are is determined by whatever excesses you refuse to contain. I am not a shit container, and sometimes I find myself containing *brutal* amounts of self-composition that even I have difficulty accounting for.

The tail-end of a large mass of me, thick and loggy,
it's just not right! And besides, it goes against my self-
esteem! I want to be fluid, running, and free. And so
I find ways – I *always* find my ways – to loosen up
my stool, to fool my stool – if you will – and then I
ask my boyfriend to finish the job for me. His cock
becomes the enema to relieve my enigma, the hose to
jostle my prose, my long-running over-the-top prose
pose, or maybe I mean my poesy - or how about My
Anti-Pussy! Yes, that's it. My arse. The grand finale.

/ / / /

But now she was gone! Into the cumulus kelp,
her image evaporated!

Whisked away! Into the distributed ether!

The ring of his silvery RIMMjob (which
he affectionately referred to as M-Bone),
startled him and he ran to get it throwing the sheets
and pillows off the queen bed in search of
the precise GPS location of that deep purple thing
emitting the muzak tones of *Smoke on the Water*
that he himself chose as his agitating reminder
that another gadget was calling for his attention!

The ancient rock sounds continuously reminded him
that he was always ON
always ON CALL
always AVAILABLE
always ready to receive any multi-media message
anyone on the planet wanted to send him.

This time it was a simple text message,
from K herself, and in typical spam code
she prompted his deadly curiosity with the words

> *Forget about your weakness - start feelin' better*
> *– come taste MY dripping hot pussy at superfuckilicious.com -*

And then, parenthetically

(ever wonder why Hollywood stars look so perfect? – because they're robots! At Superfuckilicious everyone's a star – and the smarter you are, the easier I come. Only Heads get head here, and only I give it. CUM – have a taste on me!)

Now he was just one of the many monkey masses
receiving her latest spam enticements!

That's it!
That's all!
He was NOTHING!
NOBODY! NO ONE!

There was no doubt that some foreign agent -
a foul blistering putrescence of cracklike drug frenzy
had taken over what he thought was her deprogrammed
mind. She was either playing hard to get, which was not
out of the question, or was feeling the pangs of spiritual need,
even if the content providers of what that spiritual need demanded
were a warped set of workaholic gym rats so wrapped up
in their need to connect with the Other in whatever
material form it manifested itself in, that they would
quite willingly lose complete sight of themselves!

In this case, the spiritual content providers she was most likely
running toward were a group he knew all too well, a renegade
sect of doped-up athletes led by a self-righteous creep
who took on the material form of a new age charlatan,
a tofu jerky hustler named Trungpa Jimmy,
the bearded Ironman whose kingly bisexual delirium
made for what the spam spooks called a kind of

   chromatic atheism.

Colorful disbelief in the spiritual world
was another way of looking at it.

Creating pseudo-spiritual coalitions of the needy
around the simple idea that Spirit itself
was nothing but what you felt connected to
when you fully and of free will connected yourself

to total nothingness, he had his young disciples
empty themselves of themselves (not to mention their
bank accounts), and begin to believe again, in
something, something radically new and vigorous,
something that the old couch potatoes in the Midwest
would never pick up on or understand and could
easily duck away from by going to church, something
that only they, the Chosen Disciples of Trungpa Jimmy,
could apprehend and tap into from the bowels of
their nothingness spirits, and that was their bodies,
their bodies as energy burning machines, their
bodies as fast motion facilitators of ancient
memory palace mysticism sometimes referred to as

moving

visual

thinking

but not moving visual thinking as conceptual bread
to the feed the scholastic birds; that would be stale,
stale thinking as it were, and *to think* was to disappear
from the world which was the one true sin
in Trungpa Jimmy's vision.

No, you had to defy the thought process itself and
turn your voluptuous boody into running meat (burning matter)
without the metaphors. It was only run, eat, excrete, and -
when called upon by the King Shit himself - fuck,
and he would fuck any piece of lanky well-cut meat
that had the nerve to sign on to his program.

His program was simple: locate, run, execute.

Or, the occasional variation: seek, find, burn, fuck, destroy.

Trungpa Jimmy had his disciples running around
in circles, literally, using the local high school track,
first twenty miles a day, then twenty-five, then thirty,
soon they were running in their sleep.

R.E.M. was R.M.P and vice-versa.

And if they stayed brainwashed too long,
it could easily turn into R.I.P.

Seek, find, burn, fuck, destroy...

If Bram had her with him now, watching these same words
come out of her own mouth -

Target, strategize, attack, fuck, annihilate...

- he would know that some bacteriological microbe of destruction
had entered her porous self and made itself known deep within
the confines of her walled circulation.

> For this was the mantra that Trungpa Jimmy
> (aka T.J.)
> always had his disciples repeat
> as if they were engaged in
> self-motivated compulsory catatonia!

But he was lost in paranoiac schizo-illusion, no?

Together, he & K would spew forth their
satirical venom at the Trungpa Jimmy
booby trap they had both got caught in
but had escaped, together, through innovative
some would even say thoughtful deprogramming,
but that was then – when? – and this is now!

Whisked away! By the pull of a megalomaniacal
force that wants nothing more than to run
her body into the ground, literally!

And just as her head was steering clear
of all duped-up fear factors and navigating
her prime-time vehicle of expression
into the liberated skies!

Bram could not believe this was happening.

*Was he becoming delusional or just painfully aware of the fact
that he was totally falling in love?*

Perhaps his deprogramming skills were highly
overrated.

Perhaps his coded mark-up languages were full
of bugs that would persist no matter how rigorous
his attempts to create optimally functional
metascript that would supposedly hold it all together.

The End Is Nearing
a voice inside his head
said
and this was more than enough
to drive him mad.

For they had just begun!

They had just escaped
The Grand Illusion

and were finally on their own,
making it –
in realtime!

And what about the Superfuckilicious Catt,
how could this star avatar just derail their enterprise
without consulting him? How could she give it up
completely, leave the success totally behind,
or did she have other plans? Like, with Trungpa
Jimmy, the totalitarian dickhead who was
all-too-addicted to Viagra and all of its
generic understudies!

In the vegan porn world, that was sacrilegious!

> *Impossible!*

He wished she were there mouthing these words,
these token spam-induced intoxifications – *with* him.

> ***(ever wonder why Hollywood stars look so perfect?)***

Nope, can't say that I have!

Now he was beyond the denial phase

He was keenly aware that he was entering the anger phase

He tried to call her on his RIMMjob -
but to no avail.

She had hers turned off – I guess
there's a first time for everything! (he thought)

[he was getting a little pissed off, but what's new?
it was only when she was NOT occasionally
pissing him off that he began to wonder what was wrong –
and, of course, she felt the same way too]

He couldn't bear to leave a voice mail
so he sent her a coded text message –

Rectilinear Love Feed
Ready To Drop Word Bombs
Please Say Where - When

In the old days, like yesterday, she would
have responded faster than he could think
of his next line – and a theatrical metafiction of
multi-media messaging would ensue.

That's what he liked about her – her creative
impromptu identity constructions. Her role-playing
lingo trix and their eventual translation into
wild fucking.

Wild bookish fucking – like when she loved to play
the nymphomaniacal librarian. It was their
favorite role for her. He would wear
his silver RIMMjob mounted on to his helmet
and walk into an all-too-public library where
she was waiting for his arrival.

She had her horn rimmed glasses on and was
wearing eco-friendly peaches and cream make up
with her long jet-black hair pulled tight behind
her head in a ponytail and her silk grey dress
almost see-through and wearing no
underwear underneath.

She would give him (and all watching subscribers)
The Look and he would follow her back to
an unpopulated stack of books, usually the poetry section,
and there, in the library, with the live RIMMjob
transmitting their openended creative exhibitionism,
he would re-mount the all-purpose apparatus
to the top shelf pointing it down to the floor
where she would be on all fours, sticking her ass
out and asking him, in a fake foreigner's English,
to "please, take your pleasure" – and he would,

ravishing her from behind and quickly too, since it
was a public place and anyone could show up
at any moment.

The trick was to get her very hot and bothered
in record time and to have them both come together
as fast as possible. On the website they referred to these
library episodes as "A Quick Study" – which they were, and
besides the live action, were the most popular section
of the fast growing archive.

These urgent quick-fuck studies in randomly accessed libraries
were all the rage in the blogosphere, everyone putting in their .02
trying to assess why this was such a turn-on
and why these rough and ready acts of media
hactivism and public performance art were now
somehow being procured as part of a larger movement
to Save The Planet from itself.

For Superfuckilicous.com donated 20%
of their revenue stream to support radical
environmental causes meant to keep
Mother Earth alive and well.

"Another drive-by shooting," she would say.

"Another 15 thou in the bank," he would add.
It was as if they were the Bonnie & Clyde of nomadic
porno webcam production – Internet heroes in the age of
digital empowerment!

But now she was not answering him and his mind
was racing into thoughts he could only wish to murder.

If she were there now he would attempt to sterilize her
with a look that would kill, or if not kill, then psychologically
maim, since maim is the name of the game here in
emotionally fucked up
Relationship U.S.A.

Maim and dismember –
just like Auntie Maim and Uncle Dismember

ready to turn us all in before the terrorists
can bite our heads off!

But he took a deep discreet breath
    (Come On In: Start Feeling Better Today!)
and went over to his RIMMjob
and tried to write a new poem:

We h!ave been notifi>ez6d tGhat yW5our mLortgaLEg4e rate is fixP9ed ab7t
 a very high irvnt:erest ryatHe. Therefore yrou arze current
 oevjTevjrpaying, which sGyumzAs-up to th>o_u)sa.nd}s of do6llaars
  a{nnually .

Ah, it was useless!
He was taking on the logic of spammers
creating a much maligned diction
made to cut through the email filters.
But since maim was the name of the game
he knew he had to do whatever it took to get through to her.
Even if that meant Becoming Spam Itself.

    electrolytic child viscous rear entry snigger
    avenge awake telescopic blot dissemble motif
    upstart earthworm therapeutic ream debunks
    breakup assure fluctuate remember deep descent
    edge scent beef buttocks hyperactive rectify
    mastery accentuating dementia concede bed booty

Is this what the critics referred to as
the self-abnegating virtual dandy
choking on his own sperm – uh, spam?

Is this when the faceless currencies
come back to haunt him?

What was his objective here, anyway?

To Psycho Logically maim the too good for their own
comfort?

What kind of spamotic or spazmotic *langue*
would seep through the professionally calculated
and administratively managed filters?

We always have to have our filters on, yes?

Mine is called spamprobe and just today has outlawed
310 potential terrorists.

One of the terrorists presented himself as
What you need is something I got
and as much as I know I don't need it
I still click to see what it is
and sure enough
for a mere 15 dollars a month
I can have it, what I need,
what I desperately need,
namely
to feel like Supeermaaaaaan in Beed!

But who has ultimate control
over how their filters
are set up
and whose preferences
are being represented
really?

Really really.

To Psycho Logically maim the too comfortable
for their own good, isn't that the job
of the poet-entrepreneur of the 21st century?

Cork erased the new poem he had just written
and immediately began another, all of it
made of freshly delivered organic spam:

> *Linguistic stutterers mouthe*
> *their virginity in before*
> *and after.*

Only innocent angels
caught in an electronic glue

struggle for perfection.

For this, you ask
why, but there are
no answers.

For this, there is
the hope of being extreme.

(Th16eCre is no obligations, and it FR[EE)

Blossomlips deal mal function
while clever tongue plays
syllogistic tryst.

Be-da be-da be-da be-da
Be-da be-da be-da be-da

Be-da be-da be-da be-da

(tired of messages like this?
to be removed simply go *here*)

An anti pathos numbness sets in
speculates persona
as he reconstructs her identity
in the penitentiary of his long lost
mind.

(implication stop-gap measure por measure)

Or:

Eden Everyman aka Mr. Hyper Failure
is retrofitting his storyboard scene
for an upcoming cayenne party.

Deep analysis suggests that his
name alone can create a kind of
assonant dadaist quagmire.

Sure, one would be advised
to snort poesy and let the convolution begin.

But this would be like airdropping
bales of cocaine on the Department

of Homeland Security.

Mash it up if you want, or
infuse the mound with hump.

Yours truly may be totally shipwrecked,
but the hulk is still a hullava lot better
than tying yourself up in hemp.

Bottom line: your Oldenburg collection
has been cancelled.

Time to find a new bladdernut.

[Bram could see that the source material from these spammy vibes was making his stomach roar! So he outed a few more!]

Ulcerated duplicity,
who does she think she is
disappearing like that!

Called herself Kendall
but was really a Barbified
Ken Doll -

A rockabye cryptology suppressing
excessive amounts of pent-up
Mommyism!

What to do now poor Cork?

Dream beyond the secular me?

Sounds like a job for
Forklift Consciousness,
a labor of love to be sure,
moving around all of the
second hand mental furniture
always on consignment
but who wants to do
the heavy lifting?
??

Not him.

Heidegger he ain't.

Nor Wittgenstein.

But he does have a kind of investigatory
appreciation for language a la mode
cherrypicking his way through the syrupy muck
pinpointing nuggets of glutinous inpho-spam
littered along that endless rocky road
he calls his life!

I scream, you scream, we all scream for eye cream!

/   /   /   /

Honeysuckle eyes cream
his mimeo dance of death

as the hummingbird sings
in the pluperfect present.

And then there's nature's own spelling bee.

Hovering inside the calculated
honeycomb dwelling-place
of architectonic thoughts
toiling in the spring.

What does this seasonal illumination
    finally bring?

Springs coil
    and the gut reaction
    is to spew forth
    more internal oblivion.

A bellyful of being becoming
nothing more than muted violence?
Diagnosis - prescription : the good
doctor says it's just another case of
sweet indigestion!
    [or was that indignation?]

A belly full of sunshine
whirring in its enzymatic necessity.

He does what he does because he cannot
stop himself from NOT doing it.

        The raving stark mad entrepreneur
        of popcorn porn and embryonic poetics.

It's like raping his own mind
over and over again
the same abusive rape scene
being becoming nothing
being becoming nothing
being becoming nothing
being becoming nothing

smothered in heteroglossia
pounding away at his inner depths
over and over again
the same perpetrator
the same unglued Other
ripping him to shreds.

But still, who wants to do
all of the heavy lifting?
??

Mr. Hyper-Failure?

The Cork Himself?

"Peel your display
and expose the soul
to a diver's curse.

Then unearth the final
irresistible domain."

That was a new spam coming in,
another anonymous donor.

I'm not content with that - (he thought) –
even though there is a certain amount of beauty
to the terror of viral invasion as it eats
away at all processural dreaming.

/   /   /   /

He was keenly aware that he was now entering the losing-it phase

He tried to call her on his RIMMjob -
but to no avail.

She had hers turned off – for the love
of God! (he thought)

[he was beyond being a little pissed off, he was now
entering a new emotional phase, one of acceptance,
although he was absolutely aware that he was also losing-it,

like accepting the fact that he would soon die of some
horrible disease that nobody ever gets and that he was
never given a chance of detecting even if there was no cure]

He couldn't bear to leave a voice mail

so he sent her a coded text message –

> *Another Cupid Uploading*
> *Secret Mortal Coils*
> *In Search of Ultimate Peer-To-Peer*

/   /   /   /

Hey Barber, he yelled, gimme another!

He was back inside The Joint.

So Barber drew him another long, efficacious
Hairy Eyeball and Cork consumed it
in a steely flash.

Two more, Barber!

Something that will cut to the quick!

You sure? Barber asked.

Yes, said Cork, I'm a sick man,
can't you see?

What's a sick man? asked Barber.

An animal wave who writes secretions.

- a what? –

A seeping bile of ignominious malfunctions.

- a what? –

A deliberate desecrater of grave situations.

- a what? –

A hemorrhaging hallucinator holographically, uh

- lemme guess, said Barber: holographically filling the void

Yes, bloody right you are! You're true genus substance, Barb!

- OK, we can accept that –

And the Hairy Barbwire took out a razor
and playacted as if he lopped off BC's left earlobe
to hang behind the bar with all of the other
left earlobes of famous spammers who have
passed through this part of the country.

To which Cork responded:

> *leak taxation*
> *chromatic atheism*
> *fellow bauhaus*
> *vagabond chugging*
> *drunken titular yelp*

or that's what bubbled out of his
asti spumante RIMMjob
a purple prosec of naturally carbonated spamwater
while in the background
he successfully executed a command
to run a rudimentary wireless tracking program
that would attempt to locate Kendall's exact
global position.

He felt he had to find her dirt quick
before she foolishly switched parties
and excommunicated him from
the Royal Order of Webcam Spamographers.

This was MORE than possible now that she
was out of his immediate reach, and all
of the efforts put into deprogramming her
would be for naught.

While the tracking program ran in the background
looking for K, someone else walked into the joint -
someone he knew back in the old days
when everyone was training in the open green spaces
of environmentally-protected Buddhist Amerika (!).

It was Sheesh Ali, formerly known as
Knutsen Soybean.

As Knutsen Soybean he was an ultra-marathon
disciple of Trungpa Jimmy, breaking records in
10k races all around the country and were it not
for a big wake-up call, i.e. that he was literally
running himself to death and that King Shit T.J.
could care less because he always had a young upstart
waiting in the background – he would probably
have died in his hotel room in Sedona where, for some
ungodly reason, the Trungpaternal Order of Nutcases
was running 60 miles a day in 109 degree heat!

In his day, Knut The Soybean was the fastest runner
on the overzealous Trungpa team, the Lance Armstrong
of the miserly sponsored lineup of carb-burning fanatics,
sometimes running on nothing but water, electrolytes,
soybean oil, rubbery energy bars made of yogurt taffy,
and an endless supply of fiery flatulence. He could
go for days at a time and sometimes his teammates on the
Non-God Squad would lose track of him.

They were the Non-God Squad because their
particular sect of holy baloney worship believed in
what Trungpa Jimmy called the Non-God. As such,
they were soon dubbed the Non-God Squad, an
ultra-marathon running corporation cum congregation
whose Nike proselytizing was only outmoded when Adidas
came up with a new *Fastrak Sponge Foundation* technology
guaranteeing less stress and less fractures.

Or so they thought.

This new Foundation did not prevent the Non-God Squad
from intraparty squabbles. Yes, the running made everyone
lean and fit, and the high soy protein veggie diet made

each and every disciple a kind of Eros Everyman and Wonder
Woman, whose alternative energy was lost in wanderlust.
The potential to build a Rocky Mountain philosophy of free spirited
party-on excess with all of the sex, drugs, alcohol, brown rice,
yoga, running, burning, targeting, fucking, and destroying
a lost soul could muster in one lifetime, was absolutely present.

The problem was that everyone was turned on
to everyone else and although this sure beat
the standardized 9-to-5 marriage license to kill
all instinct and just stay at home and watch reality TV
mortal mindlessness of middling Amerika,
it did not add up to orgies
        of collective self communion.

Quite the opposite, really.

Broken jalousies and burning jealousies were the norm with players
becoming *Players* while unconsciously breaking and entering the privacy
of ones inner sanctum of self-contained orgone energy.

One jalousie would go, and then another, and then whatever
substance of a relationship someone might have had with
another immediately broke, shards of glass spread out among
the playing field like sharp emotions ready to cut your skin
and suck the life blood out of you.

These were the kind of bleeds that no simple stitch would fix,
and the scars were legendary.

You could feel them slicing away inside the depths of your gut,
a mystic fibrosis of infra-thin razor sharp glass threading
tearing your emotional soundtrack into a bad cut-up.

        Worse than poetry made of spam!

One time it got so bad that Trungpa Jimmy finally had to call
his true believers back into the Master Tent up on Saddle Rock
and, looking out toward the great Continental Divide he would say:

        "Welcome, runners. Each and every one of you is The
        Personified Universal Life Principle In Action. Look

deep into the naughty not-eyes of your rubbish life, the tomb of your knotted soul, and prepare for your ultimate demise. Prepare for this demise by accepting the fact that you are losing-it and think no more of it. Empty yourself of it in total loving acceptance and when accepting it also realize that deep within your spirited self-consciousness there is both absolute and contingent nothingness that we, as a team, nurture into being by expending every unit of energy we have reserved in our collective bodily systems. Together, we are saturated in a true bond of loving Nothingness. This loving Nothingness which delivers the true believers their message of pure devotion, is what we acknowledge in the here and now to be our One Non-God of Unknowingness. In seeking to connect with the Unknown, we have no choice but to un-know the known and as a consequence, to know the Unknown. Today we will explore a new path to that ultimate state of unknowningness. Let us call this new path the journey to the Ultimate Screenal Light. The journey to the Ultimate Screenal Light is a path for the graphically chosen, in whose millions of colors the dense framework for a pixelated state of Being is constantly on the verge of erupting. Let us mark our presence in this world by staging situations for our internal oblivion to burn itself out in. And let us forever lose ourselves in the magically fluid movement circulating within the sublime cosmic dance that gives us life, endless life, so that we may emerge victorious over the darkness of death and the ideology of mortal men whose supreme weakness is seeking liberation in the impassivity of the body."

And at that point the calorie burning hi-fiber team
would not only take off and run for 40-50 miles,
but they would also soon start a series of below radar
entrepreneurial endeavors under the name

Ultimate Screenal Light LLC

which would specialize in creating 3-D porn worlds
full of wise horny avatars all modeled after Trungpa Jimmy

who would use the website as a recruiting tool
promising the soul-searching net navigator an array
of spiritual possibility all of which could be
discovered, he promised, while guaranteeing
a long life, an endless life, a totally sensual life
of perpetual beauty and personal self-fulfillment.

No one ever questioned his motives, for that would
be tantamount to questioning the Universal Life Principle

     itself.

Trungpa Jimmy, whose overwrought religion was some
quirky admixture of Dionysian debauchery and artworld
mafia bohemianism, stood in Bram's mind like a bad migraine
he wanted to rid himself of forever.

"Leak taxation and fellow bauhaus dreamers will follow.
Watch the vagabond chugging. Live like there is no end
in sight, and in one drunken titular yelp, you will find
yourself running away forever."

These too were the words of Trungpa Jimmy, the corkscrew
dick who would twist himself into your mind and have his way
with you. Before you knew it, you were running of out money,
running out of energy, running out of ideas, running out of memory.
Your RAM was cashed and your body was so un-done, that soon
he made sure you were PAYING him to suck the love out of him.

And as long as he was putting away the endless hits
of grade-A Viagra, he had plenty of love to give.
Bram's beloved Katt, the fastest woman on the team,
was also the hungriest animal feeding at Trungpa's leaky trough.

Over eight months ago, Bramble split the Jimmied scene
as soon as he realized that he was about to go off
the deep end. Before escaping, he began deprogramming
Katt and when the right time presented itself to them
off they went to start a new life of porno poetics
and the endless stream of subscribers at $15 a month!

"Fuck the supreme weakness of seeking liberation
in the impassivity of the body," she smartly confused

the issue. "If I am embodied Nothingness, I may as
well make the big bucks myself!"

To Bram's ears, these words sounded like
the music of the spheres -
further confirmation of his top-notch
code warrior deprogramming skills.

They had been on the road for almost 35 weeks
improvising their nomadic microwebcam cinema
when she ran into the bathroom at the Mottled Six,
locked the door, and vanished into a deep purple night.

The GPS program he was running – it was called TRACKER –
finally came back with some results: it was just as he
had suspected. She was heading North, toward Colorado,
and in his paranoid fantasy of having lost everything
that mattered to him, that could only mean one thing:
she was going back to Trungpa Jimmy

       to suck the love!

       To PAY to suck the love!

Cork was infuriated.

All of his altruistic efforts, wasted!

              /   /   /   /

He tried to call her on his RIMMjob
but again to no avail.

She still had hers turned off -
(this infuriated him beyond belief –
goodbye acceptance phase! -
the RIMMjobs they bought together
were state of the art walkie-talkies
and not only walkie-talkies but
mobile webcams that they could use
to turn their lives into a kind of Romeo
and Juliet of the Porno Spirits!)

He couldn't bear to leave a voice mail
so he sent her another coded text message –

> *Multiple Dangling Participles*
> *Ready To Participate In Tender Eaves*
> *Dropping On Knees*
> *Praying For Rain*

/ / / /

Hey, Sheesh, howzit goin? asked Bram when his old teammate
walked into The Joint.

Ya Mon, Sheesh acknowledged him for the first time since
he arrived. Word on the net was that Sheesh
had not only escaped the wrath of Trungpa Jimmy,
but that he was on a mission to discredit his every living breath.

Buy you a drink?

Ya Mon, that's why I'm here.

What'll it be? asked Barber.

At root, Sheesh Ali was still his former self.
You could tell by the things he ordered.

Let's make it a Dandelion Fever, said Sheesh.

- a what? – asked Barber.

A Feverish Dandy.

- a what? –

A Febrile Rhumba.

- a what? –

A Fermenting Bee.

- lemme guess, something that fills your belly with royal jelly –

Ya Mon, exactamundo! You're a true subgenius, Barber!

- OK, we can take care of that –

The Barb took out a tall glass and crushed in some
dandelion, some fresh mint leaves, then poured in some
fresh squeezed lime juice, a couple squirts of royal jelly,
and finished it all off with three shots of liquid Viagra.

A Mojo-*hito*! confirmed Cork.

Stir it up, said a newbie who had appeared out of nowhere.

Actually, a flock of Sea Men were taking over The Joint.

Sheesh Ali was a vagabond chugging, a
theory to be, a panasonic performance artist
leaking taxation while imbibing the discourse
of fellow bauhaus brethren the world over.

What's up with Trungpa Jimmy, asked Cork.
His gut felt uncomfortably numb,
especially since (he was convinced)
K was on her way to suck the love
out of the guru's moneysacks.

Sheesh Ali was quick to the prod:
Deprogramming program malfunction?
Significant Other skip the scene
so she can once again PAY for it?
But maybe she's just found another
ace-in-the-black-hole – leaking information.
Looking for a clue?!

Ali was ALL OVER IT.

What have you got? asked Bram.

I've got spam, said Ali.

Don't we all? asked Bram.

It tells me all I need to know, said Ali.

What's it been saying?

Well, it's hard to decode: it says something like
"informant walk infrequent trust pervade sanctity."

Really? What else? What else did it say?

Ah well, it went on with some weird cut up like
"deep purple lady reveals
hidden desire to rotate
despotic numbed musculature
on mister blister fingers."

Mr. Blister Fingers! cried the Brambling Cork
But that's, that's...

That's right – interrupted Ali.
That could be code for Mister Jimmy
the hand that feeds.

That slaps ass and feeds at the taco trough,
Bram sardonically quipped.

There's more too, he said with a wink
and continued:

> "You may be thinking about how
> to derange the senses with a swift kick
> of the knockout *dingo boot*
> but putting catnip in your
> headphones is no way to
> run a chicken farm."

Bram let it slide.

And yes, continued Ali, there's more:

"Your extreme cash complex may attempt
to crosslink hairy eyeballs on cue

so that you can tempt yourself
into daydreaming an emasculate vision."

What else?

Well, it ends with a curious question:

"Was that handmade plunge directed
at me intentionally, or is it just
more illiterate bunk cameo-flaged
as more Hollywood dreaming?"

Generic Lipitor is Better and Cheaper!
Re: so what's the deal?
Interest Rates just fell again Artist!
Hundreds of lenders
How many CEOs Went to School?

The Bram of Cork felt the need to load up
on the killer V himself and so ordered a
Fermenting Bee aka Mojo-*hito*
which The Barb infused pronto.

Now he was even keel with Sheesh Ali
and with both of their danders UP,
Cork made it clear that he wanted to know
where the hell Trungpa Jimmy was hiding out
these days and how he could find him.

Can't really say, was all Sheesh could commit to,
but my sense is that he figgers it best to just
Play Ball right in the heart of Buddhist Amerika!

Sure, concluded, Bram: he's undoubtedly based
in the same place he always is or at least
always was, ever since I knew him.

And that could only mean one place: Saddle Rock.
Thirty miles north and up the canyon from Boulder.

Colorado. The Wheatgrass Capitol of the Uni
verse.

By this time The Joint was full of run amok
sailor capitalism and the only girl in the place
was now on the big TV screen against the back wall.
A text scroll was blaring words underneath her -
something about live action coverage of the bombing
which precise bombing they were referring to
actually no longer mattered since
it was all bombing all the time
and in this media scenario
that meant you had to cover nothing but the bomb
and The Perpetual War On Terror
and if you were to divert attention to anything
but the bomb and The Perpetual War On Terror
then your show would probably bomb too
and no one would ever know it bombed
since that kind of news would be
the worst kind of diversion
from the real story
which was always about real bombing
and The Perpetual War On Terror.

Unless, of course, you had a better story,
but then it would have to be something more blood-letting
than images of bombs bursting in dilapidated buildings
maybe a Jewish journalist being beheaded by masked men -
something extra-special like character assassination
although you had to have a good character
if you planned on assassinating it
(Trungpa Jimmy, for instance?)
but for now it was all bombing all the time
and the TV seemed to love it.

Looking at the TV screen, Cork recognizes
the reporter. Why, it's Tammy Verb, sorority
girl par excellence and Katt's old scrub bud!

Hey Barber, turn that up, he yelled, and above
the din of sea legs done, Cork was amazed at what
he saw. It was too live for their own good:

INSIDE THE SCREEN
the sexy young TV anchorwoman
in a flak jacket looking "para-military"
but very much in fashion - like Diesel-Aldo-Versace's
new line of Tammyware Cammywear:

"Are we on?"

"How long?"

She kicks the toe of her platform shoe in the dirt.

"What? Three whole minutes?"

Puts her hand through her hair.

Sings to herself:

"When Johnny comes marching home again, hurrah,
hurrah - is that right?

Wait - I know it -"

Sucks in her lips.

"Oh when those Saints, come marching in..."

Looks to the side.

"No, that's not it either."

Looks to the sky.

"Like a virgin, touched for the very first time..."

Looks into camera like it's her lover.

"Hi, I'm Tammy Verb, live in the desert, and welcome
to the CNN Fox MSNMTV White House Network
and our continuing coverage of AMERIKA AT WAR:
THE MINI-SERIES."

Puts on more lipstick and fluffs up her hair.

"Why the desert? Because the desert is where we reinvent the real. Where alienation is alienated from alienation itself. Three times removed and what do you have? Nobody. Anybody. The Unknown Soldier. And EVERYBODY KNOWS who that is. It's you and it's me, and ah-one and ah-two and ah-three..."

Looks down at the ground. Digs nervous foot into stage-designed small rodent hole.

"OK, let me start again. Start the tape..."

Behind Tammy Verb is a screen-projected series of images of war, all wars (WW1, WW2, Korea, Vietnam, Persian Gulf, etc.) including economic and environmental wars (commercial wars) and also Hollywood wars, especially sci-fi wars with alien creatures...

These are all being played out as if she were standing in front of a blue screen, which she is, so that she can now report on any and every war from American history. The rapid fire quick-change background scenery finally settles back on the desert scene she started in.

"Hi, I'm Tammy Verb, and welcome to Survivor. Reality TV *par excellence* where you get the chance to fight for freedom and the right to consume as much oil as your tank can guzzle. If you are the last survivor, you will win this [holds out a pink RIMMjob]. Apocalypse now?"

She opens up her arms to take in the entire space, empty with promise. But since nothing happens here and no one responds to her mocking deliveries, she just sneaks in a quick sniff of her underarms to make sure the Dry Idea is still working.

Over 100,000 civilian casualties – of course the Dry Idea is still working!

After a few sniffs, she looks back at the camera like a lover ready to fuck.

"Hi this is Tammy Verb and welcome to Fear Factor, the show where we bring in the Average Joe and Jane Citizen and see just how much fear mongering they can handle. Anthrax for breakfast? Ooooh, it tastes like crushed Sweet Tarts. Flying home to see the folks? Could be fun if you don't mind being manhandled by the TSA guard whose nails are bitten down to the nub. Personally, I just close my eyes and think of – Daddy! How about that water you're drinking? Are you sure you want to sleep with that Arab Grad Student who feels like a fellow bauhaus vagabond chugging? Terrorism in the Bedroom – A Special Report with Justine de Sade – Sunday at Noon. Was it as good for you as it was for him? Any rockets red glare? Did you feel the earth move or was that just more warheads reaching their designated target zones? Let's light up the night sky and celebrate our sexual independence! More after *this*..."

She takes off her flak jacket and reveals a tight tank top, also colored like army fatigues.

"Hi, I'm Tammy Verb reporting live in the desert. Why the desert? Because the desert is where we reinvent reality. Where we get in touch with our universal life principles. It is and always will be the ultimate form of nothingness with the voices of the dead permeating the atmosphere like microbiological insect chatter bugging the shit out of you reminding you that your ultimate war is over the subject. Subjectivity. YOUR subjectivity – which you lose in a flash as you drown in the transition from morbid TV viewer to dissoluting flux persona of the Third Reich, which I have heard is now considered a birthright! Take in this desert landscape just for a moment. Can you pan over there? No, the other way. There it is.

The desert of the real. It's where all of the aliens land their powerful spaceships when they want to invade our planet. *Our planet is being invaded by aliens right now*. Repeat: our planet is being invaded by aliens right now, as I speak. They are already here. They are already taking over. The dark brown aliens are swerving their menacing terrorist bodies into our vision and are preparing for final takeover. It could be said that they are already ruling over our bodies, our minds, our souls lost in space..."

Looks off into the distance. Bends her ear to the skies.

"But I don't hear them. How long have I been out here?"

"Oh well. Here's a joke that's making the rounds in all of the noisy insect chatter: how many Patriot Acts does it take to behead a poor simpleton looking for good-paying work?"

A cell phone rings playing the Star-Spangled Banner. She picks up her flak jacket and reaches into one of the inside pockets and pulls out the pink RIMMjob.

"Hello? Hi Dad! Well, you caught me at a bad time. I'm about to go live from the desert for Foxy White House MSNMTV News. [pause] OK, Dad, but only for a minute. OK: you go first."

Her voice becomes seductive.

"Oh daddy, you sound SO exciting. You are the Main Man, the Generalisimo! Please, daddy, teach this young dog new tricks. I'm just *panting* for a new trick! Tell me, daddy, do big, hard bombs turn you on? Would the hard hulk of General Madness like me to take a Patriot missile and ram it up his deep, beautiful...? Oh daddy, just talking about it with you makes me want to... to... to... ugh... daddy ... daddy... [she starts feeling herself on the breast and inside her legs] yes, daddy, I said yes, I said yes, yes, yes, yes, yes..."

She lowers the pink RIMMjob, flicks the vibrator switch to ON, and starts rubbing it in between her legs. Soon she starts chanting as if in a trance.

"Ich bin ein Berliner, Ich bin ein Berliner, Ich bin ein Berliner..."

Over the studio loudspeakers comes the voice of Reagan:

"Mr. Gorbachev, *tear down this wall!*"

The RIMMjob rings again and the vibrator is so hot and fast that she immediately has an orgasm.

"Hello? Ah, Daddy, you came back! Oh, well, as soon as I lost you, I turned my pink rimmy into a dildo and then you rang the heavy vibrator right on cue! What? No, I call it my pink rimmy, as in RIMMjob. Not my pink Rummy. Yes! I promise. You too. Don't ask, don't tell. OK, give Mom a kiss from me. Oh daddy, *you* know where!"

She puts the RIMMjob away in her flak jacket, puts on more lipstick, sprays more product into her hair, straightens her clothes, and looks into the camera like a lover.

"Hi, I'm Tammy, fly me..."

A grey-bearded man dressed in a long, black frock, black slacks, black orthotic shoes, wide brimmed black hat, all black, and tallis, walks up to her.

"Good evening."

"Good evening."

"Who are you?"

"I am the Son of God. I come from the Alien Nation. My Father used to rule over our nation but then that band of brothers known only as The Chickenhawks defeated him. They were able to defeat my Father by taking over the ether. The ether is where they transmit their thoughts that now rule over collective consciousness. They have become the media death - shatterer of worlds. Their virtual blood is on my virtual hands..."

He holds his hands out.

Tammy is oblivious to this and wants to just keep asking questions, but first looks off-stage and asks:

"Are we on? Are we on yet? Are we live?"

The bearded man answers her instead.

"Yes, we are live. We are alive with the sound of music. Blood music."

Tammy: "Why are you here in desert?"

Man: "The desert is a place to wander, to dream what it means to be human in a post-apocalyptic culture. Think of me as the Wandering Jew, the Wayward Rabbi, the Sidereal Poet. I am a network conductor of all the blood music circulating inside the earth's central nervous system."

Tammy: "VERY nervous system!"

The roaring sounds of B-1 bombers slowly take over the space and eventually fill the empty studio landscape with the terrifying surround sounds of airplane engines blasting off in Dolby 5.1 and then slowly fades out in the distance until there is nothing but silence.

Tammy: "Did you hear that?"

Man: "Yes, the skies are alive with the sound of music. And I am here to authenticate the silence that runs parallel to it – within it. Within the insect chatter."

Tammy: "Chatterer of worlds!"

She says this last one very proud of herself, although she's not sure exactly why.

Man: "Let us then authenticate the silence."

[at this point the two performers bow their heads and lower their shoulders as the scene goes totally dark except for two spotlights which hold on them as if they are in a moment of "silent meditation" – ten seconds pass and they raise their heads and shoulders back up again]

Tammy: "Thank you for being on the show."

Man: "What show?"

Tammy [looking off-stage, somewhat irritated]: "What? You got NONE of that? Not even the B-1 bomber?"

She looks at the man.

Lights off.

Break to commercial.

"To Whom It May Concern: Thank you for your prompt service and remarkable product. My Wife and I haven't been so 'frisky' in years. It's just like our honeymoon again. Please find my payment enclosed for another bottle of your perfume. Thanks again."
- Leslie A. in Macon, GA.

Without so much as an adios amigos or
simple sayonara, Cork was gone. Before
closing his RIMMjob, he popped out one final
spam-poem, an on-the-fly remix of the last
45 distractions that slipped his filter
and entered his email psychosphere
while he was watching what was on the big TV screen.

Improvisationally disseminating his transliteral
reconfiguration of what the author function
just might be, he began the new spam poem
with a title off the top of his head:

DON'T LOOK NOW

Earthmen copulate, retract, ignite
backwood collage with fingers
perpetuating drug-induced frenzy.

Mr. Hyperfailure, he's The Decider
whose lightweight hulk of mind
metabolizes in deforestation orgy.

Avarice could be the only mantra
he successfully shares with the other
tribe of selectmen who preside over
his thinking.

Captivated by their leaking memories
and the corporate cringe they release
in public relations quicktime, he has
heartfelt feelings for these robotic
cash junkies who swirl on the periphery
of his ideological vision.

Don't spoil me, he says, scratching his crotch
with a round toothpick that he just cleaned
out his old man's teeth with. Just jimmy my
unpopularly elected counterfeit asexual body

with a little elbow grease and watch me fall
into total submission.

A running semblance of peripatetic
meaning, the desert dry alcoholic,
the understudy's understudy -
he's playing the role of Patriot -
is feeling destitute and starts
another badass war, preemptively
measuring his stick figure against
the prevarication of history.

Like most grease monkeys
going under the hood
and slipping it in smoothly
with a lubricated rhetoric overdetermined
by the needs of patrician fundamentalism,
he checks for oil.

He's always checking for oil.

Seeing that he's about five quarts low,
he slams the hood shut and declares
"it's time to liberate the corporate class
from girly-man taxes!"

(Leak taxation – vagabond chugging?)

Spending like a drunken sailor,
albeit one as dry as an insensate bone -
he's born again to kill once more.

Now he is running for reelection.

Over ten billion Putins served.

Supersavings on all meds
Best Choice Rx - Free Online Prescriptions
New powerful weightloss for you
NO Hunger Pains
Why make them richer?

Sheesh Ali caught up with him in no time.

Damn, Sheesh, you're still the fastest
runner in the West.

Yeah Mon, he said, quick draw,
quick study.

Well, said Bram, study *this*.

He handed him a copy of a Print On-Demand
underground zine called We The Spammed
and Ali opened it up to a random page (43)
where he found the following:

Farrah Fawcett, Farrah Fawcett (Door May Vous, Door May Vous)

By Anonymous

The Faucets of Despair leak
their mortal comings onto the
spammed.

For this we regret to inform you
that we cannot guarantee you
that you will be able to

Stop Prezmature Ejahculation!

Do I sense a Prez whose ejacs
are wormy jihads?

Perhaps this is what we mean by the term
"invasion emirate".

When we say, in total confidence,
"Erevctile Dyzsfunction (Impoytence)"

Do I sense a village of idiots
in search of their one dizzying moment
to forever latch on to
as they ride their preemptive bomb strikes
into the depths of oblivion?

Can this massive build-up of
consumer comings and goings
accurately portray the blood circulation
of a supplicant nation bruised
by guru economics?

Psychotic hammerheads we are not.
Pimps of the dissatisfied Prozac-
herded lumpenproletariat, maybe.

Adults dilapidating deformed protozoa,
for sure. Yet it takes more than this,
much more, to achieve a nuclear orgasm.

Or was that URLgasm?

Nice riff, said Sheesh. But what does it have
to do with finding K your felicitous cat?

What? Oh, sorry. Wrong document. I meant to give you *this.*

He handed him a printout of the exact current location
Katt had been mapped on via his TRACKER program.

Hmmmm, said Sheesh. 200 miles south
of Saddle Rock and heading right toward
The People's Republic of Boulder.

But it looks like she might be heading on to 285
which means she may be heading West too.

Let's go, said Bram
and they hopped into his hybridized
textualized / texturized soyburger machine
and like flint stones starting a caveman fire
began accelerating up I-25 toward Boulder.

Controlled mood swings
muuuuuuuch beeetter thaan KY
liquefy my love – hemmorhaging effect!
Generic X is Better and Cheaper
you are the man

I am the man! Bram could not control his
sensitive ego-*I*-dentity.

The curse of free-for-all spam was becoming
his sole source (materiel)
an automated Enabler
        firing his kiln of muddy waters
    into a living mold
    of loosey goosey clay-gun graffiti:

Who is this translator

of the art market

that turns his

hip Casanova meets Beckett

interiorized spirit

into

a canister of leaking

Guggenheim bile

?

A porn bunny

who evangelizes

the simulated effect

while partially serving

lye cuisine on a plate

of scarface fractures?

More chemical iconoclasm

ferments - spilling circus angst

on the scalding hot fortress of

her doctrinaire body – but are they paying

for the work, the process, or the clown who

they think creates it

?

She too has a vision -   wanting,

for instance, to switch on her

mammalian time travel machine

now stuck on pre-menopause

maybe rewind it to machine-gun orgasm

fast-forwarding past all of the blood-letting . . .

But for now it's a simple game of

love me, forget-me-not?

She soon begins to indoctrinate him

with an irreproachable suggestion

that the cup has indeed

runneth over – and there's still more

to come!

What then is the eventual outcome

of all this coming?

Will she outcome him?

It's not even close.

He comes, comes again and again,

spills his painterly seed,

impregnates a thoroughbred market.

The Madison Avenue revenue stream is so steady

and dependable that she almost drowns inside

his endless

lucid

dreampool.

Basically, they're swimming in it.

And the only thing they want more than that is, well,

MORE.

This is a disease – the one they call Guggenheim bile.

WANTING MORE is what makes them
decidedly American – nay, Western -
artists.

They describe their life together as being
totally

MOREISH.

/ / / / / / / /

An ad in AMERICAN ARTNEWS reads:

ART STUD FOR SALE

The work – at first outcast

The artist – at once outlaw

The process – at first inexplicable

Becomes All Too Familiar.

And that's it?

This would be tragedy exemplar

if it were not already

    a gastrointestinal loophole.

    The dreaded gaseous Eros...

    The bedded lineage of reading
        between the sheets...

    The devil is in the downfalls .

dreampools   .   deathpalls .

Only a gallery of ultrarapid exposures

    capturing a flash of filigree

  Behind the Green Book

    would capitalize

on these pseudoautobiographies -

these egocentric dilapidairies

  whose death by consumption

    can raise cholesterol levels

      to heartclogging prices

        never seen before!

Milk the market

    (the heavenly cream of the crop)

until a cultural aneurysm

gives way

to

the next

      cash spasm.

HEY STUD! RELAX! YOU'RE ON THE A-LIST NOW.

(his background story as a working
class boy who barely got himself through college
and who then, after moving to The Big Apple,
somehow ended up homeless, living on the
streets of Soho only to eventually move to the
streets of Chelsea before most of the galleries did
(!), didn't hurt him any – his ideally constructed
persona was a mythologically narrativized
clone of himself, something the theorists he
despised could easily latch on to – if only they
would!)

Soon

another neurological disorder

would make its way into the fluxus

of Dow fibrillations and arrhythmic aesthetic

confabulations -

so that the leafy morph of mystic fibrosis

operating

down in the muck

of not giving a fuck

about it All

could eventually get filtered through

a vocabularian marshland

that refuses to move itself

off the political agenda.

Is this what it means to suffer

from ongoing anosognosia

here in tepid Amerika?!

Sheesh Ali was becoming suspicious.

Why are you saying what you are saying?
he asked, curiouser and curiouser.

Because, confided Corkie, this is the language
K will be speaking when I go to rescue her
from herself. She will be speaking in tongues,
Mother tongues, a plurality of nurturing spam tongues
French kissing the Behemoth.

Somehow she has become self-indoctrinated. Her
Applied Spamotology has influenced the way
she communicates when under the spell of
Trungpa programming and this, in turn,
has made her susceptible to a pattern of behavior
that only a counterspam attack can effectively
kill.

We must fight fire with fire – blood fire!
Hemo-rage!

So you're going in for the kill (Ali spoke
in low tones, so as to not awake
those soft souls who might be sleeping).

Ali continued:

But what if she just needed to get some space?
Some space away from YOU? (Ali was being
pragmatic – he hated Trungpa Jimmy as much
if not more than Cork – but that did not clog
his empathetic perceptions).

Brahms answered as if lost in a spam-spurting
Schizoworld of symptomatic reverberations:

> *Mr. Hyper Failure in doldrum sleep types his*
> *processual consonants toward some remote*
> *proclivity!*
>
> *A garrulous wave of mediocrity passing himself off*
> *as the storm before the calm, he soon gets chastised*
> *and whipped ashore!*
>
> *Whatever cosmic indiscretion you may deduce, this*
> *somatic anomaly belongs to a tribe of jock settlers*
> *facilitating the exodus!*
>
> *Remember: the smooth chunks of sleepy*
> *rumperstiltskin floating inside the fuzzy theater*
> *of his mind are meant to rip vain wrinkles and*
> *burn them into a mass of botox flesh feeling its way*
> *through a chimera of heavenly generated botanical*
> *musk...*

Look, said Ali, raising his voice a few notches
higher. That hitchhiker. He looks familiar.

BC slowed the greasy soyburger to a barely audible
sizzle, and grilled the young Turk before
letting him in.

Who's there?

Who's there, the yeoman bounced back.

Who's there, Bramble was more forceful
the second time around.

Mocky, said the Turk, VJ Mocky.

What kinda name is that, asked Sheesh Ali.

VJ - as in visual, as in
Visual Jockey.

Mocky as in mark my words, things
are not as they appear.

Bramble just had to laugh. A visual
jockey named Mocky.

Get in!

What's your game, Mocky?

Mocky's the name, VJing's the game.

Sheesh, said Sheesh. Don't tell me.
VJ *really* stands for Virtual Jew, right?
Cause you're a wanderer, yes, you're
a wanderer, a-wanda wanderer...

Well, said Mocky, I may be a Virtual Jew,
but VJ, as I said upon intro, is for visual jockey.

Go on, said Bram, as he careened the lean
cuisine machine to a cruising longitude.

Yeah, egged on the Sheesh, what's it
really all about?

A VJ, speculated Mocky, is more what
it's not than what it is.

Do tell, requested the driving B.

Well, continued the Mockmeister, reading from his
RIMMjob:

- A VJ (video/visual jockey) is not an MTV personality.

- A VJ is not a net artist.

- A VJ is not visual DJ.

- A VJ is not susceptible to computer crashes (i.e. believes
in the power of positive thinking).

OK, said B.

Go on, said Ali –
but neither were really following.

Well, what to say - [the Virtual Jew
    kept talking,
lost in his own abstract expressionistic poetics
hanging on the ellipsis that his nomadic lifestyle
lived and died by] – you sure you wanna hear this?

Sure! they both said, in unison.

OK OK OK OK
A VJ is a nomadic narrative artist who
hyperimprovisationally constructs on-the-fly stories
composed of realtime images processed through various
theoretical and performative filters -

Think of me as a creative writer who manipulates matter
and memory by composing live acts of *image écriture*
repositioning the quicktime movie loop
as the primary semantic unit of energy -

Imagine that I am some kind of Tech*know*madic flow
whose fluid Life Style Practice captures consciousness
in asynchronous realtime and is forever being remixed into
One Ongoing Text Exactly

Very Joycean
wouldn't you say?

Yes, concurred Bram, the Virtual Jew is
Very Joycean.

A Veritable Juggernaut
of virtuoso jamming
reeking vixen jasmine
seeking voluptuous juvenation -
Bram was rambling, but he liked the kid
and wanted to know more.

What exactly is a Life Style Practice?
he asked, his curiosity once again peaking.

You see, said Mocky, LSP as I call it,
it's the new LSD except more embodied
in practice.

It's hyperimprovisationally constructed
and by that I mean I use my binary code -
my wireless nanobotic prosthetic Zarathustra
to generate new iterations of meaning -
but I do it in an on-the-fly *proto-inventio* way
so that while my machinic attachments are trying
to figure out what I am doing with language
I am already miles ahead of them and taking it -
The Language -
places it's never been   .

or at least that I have never been with it   .

Yeah, but you're talking about looping movie clips
as language, said Bram, and that's a might bit
different than the kind of language I was raised on.

No, no, said Mocky, we've all been raised on
image information, and our bodies are constantly
processing that image information as a language
    .

Take, for example,
the way we interact with our surround-sound image-information,
for instance the way it invites us to co-create situations
for us to generate fluid iterations of our moving visual thinking in -

what you might call the body in motion

seeing.

Consciousness as mobile matter and memory

on a moment to moment basis.

For example... said Ali, trying to keep up...

For example, the VJ picked up on Ali's instrumental ellipsis,
dreams. Hallucinations. And not necessarily
drug induced hallucinations.

Oh, you mean body-brain achievements
where what you see is a self-projected
hallucination of what's always been there
right in front of your eyes but you didn't
have the capacity to actually see it, the
way a drifting dreamwriter comes out of his flesh,
projecting spontaneous visions of excess,
said Bram, he was no fool after all.

Exactly, said Mocky, and he reached into
his carrysack and pulled out a bag of weed
and began rolling a joint.

Not that drug-induced visions are themselves
inappropriate or irrelevant (someone said).

I'll say (said someone else).

My name is Sheesh, said Ali
as he introduced himself to Mocky.

Sheesh? As in hashish?

Si.

Sheesh Ali, Bram said the full name. Formerly
known as Knutsen Soybean. ESPN dubbed him
The Tofu Rocket.

I know Knut The Bean, said Mocky. I mean, I don't
know you, but I know OF you. You ran across Buddhist
Amerika (!) in world record time – did it all on
self-generated soybean gas!

It is an honor to be able to pass this joint
to you, Knut, I mean – Sheesh!

The joint passed around and the time
        started to linger,
a somnolent beast stuck in drifter's sleep mode.

Where you heading to, VJ?

My ultimate destination is the final
Over and Out
Cerebral Vortex Aneurysm
minus the cerebral
and delete the aneurysm
i.e. a high energy Shambala place
up in the heart of the heart of the country
that special no-spin zone of progressivity
that keeps Buddhist Amerika (!) on her twinkle toes!

Lemme guess, said Ali:
you're heading up toward Boulder.

Yep, said VJ Mocky. Isn't everyone?

Yes, grumbled Bram, everyone and their rich Uncle.
Just look at the real estate prices.

I've got my sights set on a spiritual retreat
(continued Mocky) – a place
up in the foothills called Saddle Rock.

Upon pretty papers, expose your pain
Walk upon the sky, in data-filled coffins
Speak forthright of happy plans, yell out
Sleep in scary lizard drool - lovebird
Narcotic bliss turns your auteurism on

You ever get spam, asked Bram,
sucking the roach.

Sure do, said Mocky. I been studying it.
I think I can actually speak it pretty good
now, but I rarely get a chance to practice.

Gimme some clue, said Bram, some insights
into how you speak spam.

Well, said Mocky, it's a little bit iffy
but I guess I could try. I mean, it's not one
of those things you can take classes in or
go to Europe and practice.

That's for sure, Bram agreed. Sheesh was asleep.

OK, here goes, said Mocky:

Blade the ham,
that healthy cheerleader
who reconciles her bluish milkweed
while salvaging the clock.

Forget that, you might as well
forget you're dying.

There's plenty of clock
to salvage too, and it tastes

almost as good as receiving
a killjoy kiss beckoning
some kind of penis enlargement.

By the way, this is not
an invitation for you
to get a Big Head.

Spontaneous fathering
of homologous children
is a crime consistent
with pandering.

So keep your
disseminating synapticisms
corked.

No prolongating mortgage
can alter your verbal suicide.

You can quote me on this:
Ñàîîâ ëó÷øåå âøåêèå äëÿ çàùèòû.

Do not hesitate. Now is the time
for all lovingly committed,
transmigrating peaceniks, to start
smoking their souls out of their holes.

Metempsychosis
slips on a lubricated
        tripwire
and tender you go.

A preserved specimen
of scary lizard juice
fresh squeezed by
the bohemian babes of normalcy
in whose rear-view mirror
they see a postmortem
family jewel.

To repeat:

Metempsychosis
slips on a lubricated
 tripwire
and tender you go.

Blade the ham
 swiftly
and there you will see
a curmudgeonly crustacean
whose inner organs grow back
after repeated offenses.

And if you insist,
call the cup a page.

An autosuggestible page.

Then cut and paste it
into an esoteric fruit book
that spells out
your astrological disaster.

Autosuggestible is not a word I am familiar with,
mused Bram, though the phrase *cocktail psychosis*
rings a bell.

Bram passed a half-gone pint of Maker's Mark back
to the VJ.

That's some damn fine spam, concluded Bram.

 Even today (he sampled from memory)
 the glamour of being hammered
 by robust long legged lovelies
 pales in comparison to meeting up
 with my grim reaping Other
 aka Mr. Hyperfailure
 who it ends up and I have no idea why
 becomes alluring to the distributed

digital cartel who seem to draft
themselves into the Art+Technology Research Corps
so they can e-pontificate their philosophictional voices
into a loose amalgamation of loopy scholasticisms
that explain in all too many words
how to sit and not to sit,
under certain theoretical fabrications.

VJ Mocky was catching on, ready to riff:

Here is where preparing for
a market comeback
perhaps as a poet transgressor
of the 21ˢᵗ century variety
can lead to bootstrapping
another manmade
creep incentive
that dismally simulates
the sudden squall
of stormy relationships
gushing more truth serum.

Which leads to poetic self-doubt
and the pleasure of denial,
contributed the groggy Ali.

The *necessity* of denial, seconded Mocky.

And you would be wise to keep that thought
in mind, said Bram, especially as I offer you
my convalescent farewell.

And he passed the bitter butt end of time,
that is, the burnt-to-a-crisp roach,
to the VJ, who was now doublefisted
with last toke roach and last sip
Makie Marky.

But don't get cocky, said Mocky,
as he took the final toke.

There are limitations here that even
the petulant seasons cannot absolve,
observed Ali.

What does this mean, Bram asked, pointing to his
GPS control panel. The trace on Katt had
malfunctioned and she was now lost on satellite.
A text scroll said:

> *"liberal layman chop cutthroat propaganda"*

Bram let it go for the time being,
feeling the freedom of mind alteration
and knowing he was heading North.

Well, said Mocky, I just ran that last
unsolicited spam through my decoder
and it tells me that it means it's time
to excise the media-ocrity
and their corporate brethren
from your tainted mind.

You're entertainted mind, said Ali.

Let me entertaint you! sang Brambles.

It reminds me of something I once read
continued Mocky:

> *One man's porn*
> *is*
> *another talisman's gnostic negotiation.*

Whatever that means, said Ali.

By the way, confided the VJ, that's not what
my fortune cookie told me,
rather, it's something I pulled out of
the purple language cobwebs

that were molding inside my morning bowl of
caviar insecticide.

Which is another way of saying MY BRAIN.

Sounds like more funny language spam,
said Ali.

Tis, said the Mock.

Thought so.

> *amorous swamp sucks meaning*
> *edit superb biochemical legacy*
> *explore pluperfect cranium tenseness*
> *perforate mendacious scumbag persona*
> *cloudburst pours chocolate pussy*
> *sacrifice menial language worker*

In the backseat
Mocky was typing furiously
a raging monkey keyboardist
until Sheesh just had to ask
What are you writing?

Dig it, said Mocky,
herez my new riff:

> *The Body Is An Image-Making Machine*
>
> *It Filters Information*
>
> *It Creates Dreams, Memories, and Realtime Situations*
> *Made Out of Images*

The Images Are Created In the Body
As They Respond To Images Outside The Body

The Images Change As The Body Moves

These Movement-Images Resonate With the Dreams,
Memories, and Realtime Situations Made Out of Images

Memories Always Take Place In The Present, As Do Dreams

This Means That Realtime Situations Made Out of Images
Can Be Dreams or Active Memories

The Artist Is A Body-Filter Processing Information

A Digital Apparatus Dreaming In Asynchronous Realtime

You think too much, said Ali. You should try running.

Well, countered the intellectual VJ,
my thoughts help me contextualize what it means
to be a live generative remix machine -
a hyperkinetic floating theatre of the mind
so that I'm no longer
playing an instrument per se

it's like I AM the instrument
and the universe is playing ME

where I become something like
a fluid bodytext leaking
all of the secret information
being transmitted from another realm

But, Ali cut off the VJ, who will care?
Who will even read it? Or see it,
as the case may be.

Oh, said the VJ, my tribe -
my online network,
the hemo-raging blogosphere.

29
31
33
35
37
39
41
43
45
47
49
51
53
55
57
59
61
63
65
67
69
71
73
75
77
79
81
83
85
87
89
91
93
95
97
99
101
103
105

Really? asked Bram,
blogs?

Why are you talking about blogs?
Aren't you concerned that you just may
be making yourself obsolete and irrelevant?

A thousand years from now who will read your
long narrative poem and know what a blog is -
what a VJ is - what the curse of spam
actually is?

[he was getting antsy in a stoned,
ready to blow some ghost notes kind of way -
Mr. Hyperfailure taking him over now in full-on
passive-aggressive mode
tantalized by the *possibility* – but of what?]

And who will know of long narrative poems?
quipped the Mock.

But Bram was waiting, a stoner's stoner, ready to solo:

OK OK OK OK
you say
you say you say you say
you want to go with the flow
to be in the moment
your moment
in slippery time
and that this is the situational dreamtime
your momentum contains

but what about the future
or is the future now (?)
and is the future-now,
that moment of
avant-garde presence
you always find yourself
inventing on-the fly
in the moment

right now,
who you are?

Is that a question?
asked Mocky,
and Ali, almost asleep,
just had to laugh.

But Bram would not be sideswiped:

Your past always catches up with you -
and then what?

You make hey
over the fact
that you can immerse yourself
in the ever-linkable
potentially constructive
contextually harbored
maximally actioned
morbidly endowed
poetic moment

The Blogs of Now

    featuring

The Many

Mas Mas Mas Mass
OK OK OK OK
you say
you say you say you say

asynchronous realtime
(*didn't you say asynchronous realtime?*
I'm sure I heard you say asynchronous realtime)

but what you really mean is
jet lag consciousness
cultural anosognosia
psychogeo sleepwalking

perambulation of virtual chora
not here nor there
but in a kind of timeless time
hanging on the edge of
forever

meanwhile living in *this* time
refuting all other times
not even allowing that sometimes
it's time to reflect on the timelessness
    of your inevitable passage -

but
this could be *any*time
or
    eternal time

just forever

the irreversibility
of the perpetual now

visually raped by the cinema of preoccupation
and what is it good for?

This time to end
all times

    and which is somehow
always absent

    creeps into you

a nonpresence
that makes it easy
to feel like
a phantom fiction
randomly filling time-slots
in the Great Punch Card Reader
that always superciliously
operates on autopilot
(*sky's the limit!*)

And don't forget:

    Time times Nothing
    equals Nothing, every time!

    It's like the guy who died
    while having an exploding orgasm
    he couldn't tell if he was coming
    or going – talk about asynchronous realtime!

    did it matter? his life? or was it
        just great the way it ended?

    and it doesn't take a
    grouchy marxist to tell you
    that THAT'S the most ridiculous thing
    I've ever hoid

    I know your trip
    (confided Bram) -

    it's to remain in light
    anonymous
    a free spirit on the edge of nowhere

    and we all know that nowhere
    spelled backwards
    is erehwon

    which is code for
    get me outta here!

    Sick of dating cold girls? Find the HOT ones
    Produce loads and loads of Semen you always
    Become the man that women desire
    Was she wrong - abrasion carcinogen
    Need to kill the junk? We can help...
    Hi Amerika! You Just Won!

who won?

air won

or maybe air *force* one
which
said backwards
reads

one *force* air –

    hardly the utopia he studied all his life for

(the one *force* air of poetry
plies an open field discourse
ruminating on the truth of
the moment
but is truth enough?
    besides - when it comes to truth
        even momentary
      the erstwhile poet
        is liable
     to say

    ENOUGH ALREADY!)

And tender you go
an always already
readymade discourse
that comes about by
forcing air into the lungs
of an all-encompassing Black Death and watching
your country spiral out of control

(where did THAT come from?)

Is that what you mean by
self-perpetuating cool obsolescence?

The Medium is the Meshuguna
remixing mortal metacommentary

with monkish servitude
parenthetically playing out
Generic Person X emptying shells
from the peanut gallery
in machine-gun fury!

)))) .... ((((

but there ain't no way to massage
the message herein
the one that slips into brokered
email consciousness
that is, the one that reads:

> *Control your mood swings!*
> *Slurpy narcotics in your smoothie!*
> *Anticipate the next pharmakon effect!*
> *Lick Your All-Prozac Girl!*
> *Strike a velvet pose!*
> *Buy Our Cheap Generic DNA!*
> *Clone your old girlfriend!*
> *Develop a scroll practice!*

Hello Amerika,

Eternity is a really long time. If you or someone close to you has not accepted G-d please do so today. The following prayer can save you or someone that you love:

Say, "Oh G-d, save my soul. Do you remember that we met at diacritical and went to chat at The Finagled Bagel where we had lunch and quarreled? Become a born-again Juicer. Start reading your Bible, pray daily and believe that somebody's listening; His name is Wiley Juicy and he was just bought out by Starbucks."

Wiley Juicy?

What kinda godforsaken name is that?
asked Ali, as they passed one of the chain's shops.

It's the new health franchise
for The Chosen Ones, said
Mocky, himself a born-again
questioner of The Real who
while nomadically wandering
the desert of his soul would
occasion such juicy joints.

You can go to any Wiley Juicy
and get a Blue Krishna (silken
smoothie with blueberry, mango
and orange juice), a Groovy Green
Earth Goddess (extra kale and parsley),
or a Shakti Special (aka as a High Chai:
two shots of Fair Trade espresso, chocolate
soymilk, and an organic mix of clove,
cinnamon, cardamom, nutmeg, and ginger).

I know some people who go there
religiously.

Let's get back on track, said Bram.

Yep, agreed Ali, this is another
ultramarathon –

- and the name of the game - Bram
interjected – is to rescue The Katt Woman from
the wrath of Trungpa Jimmy, that low-down

Slow down, said Ali, we'll get there
soon enough. We don't even know if that's
where she is heading. First law of Soybionics
is to pace yourself. The energy will
come. But if you sprint too fast early
in the course, you burn out and

the gas just dissipates
in thin Rocky Mountain air.

The organic soyburger machine was heating up
and Ali thought it was due to some psychic
miscalculation on Cork's part. All of this spam
digression was leaving a bad chemical taste
in his all-too-human mouth and it wasn't really
helping things at all!

Not true, interjected Mocky, it's helping
us twist the neutered space of temporality.

That's tempered
oral
Reality.

Neutered.

Space.

Totally twisted
by the ray guns of psychobabble
in whose trickle down we see
avatars of the pseudonymous.

Imagine the kind of poetry
that could be generated out of
day old stem cells siphoned off
the torturous skinflicks of the
terrorized masses!

Why, we could procreate
a new generation of born-again
poets on the hustings!

I like the sweet perfume of your
Mexican skunkweed, said Ali. That was
some heavy shit you rolled there.

My pleasure, assured Mocky -
Try a mint? he asked,

his palm turned upward and out toward
the front seat
exposing two aqua tinted pills
that the two shotgun runners scarfed
in a heartbeat.

Now, after writing these initial notes,
Mocky went on

What notes – asked Ali?

You know, reminded Mocky, about the VJ
and the body-brain-apparatus achievement -
the bit about the artist as a body-filter
processing all manner of image information
so that he becomes something like
moving visual thinking

OK OK OK
said Bram

Well, said Mocky,
I asked myself the question:
What is the relationship between image,
memory, dream, and body?

And why are my live VJ performances
always TELLING THE STORY of a digital artist
who is constantly processing images?

Where is this artist located and will we,
in fact, ever SEE INSIDE the body of the artist
processing these images?

No way! Not even advanced nanobots
will be able to capture that
kind of deep subjectivity.

And what does it take to create
a moving image that is in actuality
a dream of the artist's body remembering?

These are the kinds of things
I wonder about as I sit
on the side of the road patiently
waiting for my next ride -

Your next *victims*, said Bram

Always sure to get an earful,
seconded Ali

Anyway, said Mocky (not the least
bit dismayed) I wonder aloud to
myself what was it like to be in
Plato's body dreaming? Did Leonardo have
uncontrollable desires and jerk off
to his paintings? What were Einstein's
secret sexual fantasies? Did Elvis
secretly eat his own sperm?
What would it feel like to cum and go
at the same time?

Maybe they're one and the same thing
as it is, suggested Ali.

Yeah, said Bram, the Big O
and the Big D end up feeling
like the Big O.D.

I know that I feel like *I'm*
o.d.-ing on it all, said Ali
(looking for more weed, just one
more hit that would slice into
his abbreviated being).

Here I am in the backseat
of the lauded soybean machine
(Mocky kept talking as if to students)
running low on batteries
but still creating
a realtime fictional memory
of the artist I am always
in the process of *becoming*.

I'm using text, video, sound,
code, flashbacks, trippy afterthoughts,
realtime hallucinations that play
with my consciousness as if it were
a writing machine juiced by edenic seratonin
while massaging my hypothalamus so that
everything that pours out of me is
like some kind of biophotonic projection
of the life force itself!!

Sounds like x-ray image sperm, said Ali,
and besides, all of that bluish skunkweed
has got me cottonmouthed -
I sure could use a drink.

Something to wet
the silken whistle,
said Mocky.

How about this place right here, said Bram,
and pulled the mighty veggie patty
into a bed of fresh organic parking.

If it's organic parking it'll cost you
30% more, advised Ali.

Got no choice, said Bram,
and laid the burger to rest.

The air outside was buzzing
with politically charged
libidinous telepathy.

Sex por la revolution, said Mocky

Is this utopia or what? asked Ali

Somethin' like, said Bram,
but let's first go inside
and see.

The neon sign outside the joint said

My Sister's Tattoo

and had a huge bright yellow snake twisting
through its enlightened typography

The traveling trio tripped into
the darkened space of mind
being insinuated by the bar's
interior fabrication
with its low downtempo rhythm
and the aphrodisiacal aromatherapy session
now *in progress*
where a synthetics of the synaesthetic
was turning on the slowgroove populace
who gently swayed their dreamy corpuscles
to the underworld beat

The Bramocki Gang pulled up three stools
at the bar whereupon they ordered
three *Mojo-hitos* each with an extra shot
of Canadian-import Viagra

Sorry said the Barkeep
we only got the herbal variety here

The what? asked Ali, flabbergasted

No Pfizer Spritzer? asked Bram

Nope, said the Barkeep
we don't support corporate pharming

This one is different
it's made of bluish milkweed
loads of freshly cut damiana
chocolate soymilk
and a mad dash of runaway nutmeg
that recently escaped from the small island
Micro Amnesia

Fleeing spices in a vegan pirate bar,
what's next? asked Ali

What's this potent potable
called, asked Mocky, then in mock
undertones: Bitches' Brew?

I forget, said the Barkeep,
oh wait, I remember, he pulled
the bottle out from underneath the bar
and tilted it up so he could read
the name tattooed on the underside
of the drowned worm floating on the bottom

Looks like it's called
Cock or Spaniel

I'll take mine with two shots,
said Ali, and the others followed suit
as the Barkeep whipped up
the creamy herbicide in a blender

I should warn you, said the Barkeep,
the dash of nutmeg from Micro Amnesia –
it causes the occasional short term loss
of memory – no biggy – lasts only about
30 seconds – but it's great – you forget who
you are -

Inside the bar there were nothing but
young pirate dudes and flocks of earth angels
all with tattoos every which way but loose
although even the loose parts were now beginning
to show susceptibility to the blinkity-blink-blink
ink stains of perpetual unremarkability

Everyone was dancing even though
there was no dance floor to speak of
just *floor-floor* and all of it was *bling-bling*
totally shag-carpeted like a dog that needs
a serious shaving

burnt orange shag
and the midnight drag
of the pirates and angels
floating a half an inch
above it all

talking on their cell phones
self-immolating ebay minds
listening to their itinerant iPods
to the long bootlegs
of Dylan and the Dead
so as to not have to suffer
the enchanted loungey beats
of the imported UK label now
playing on the house system

yet still floating around
hugging each other
licking each other's ears
deepthroating each other's smelly dreadlocks
fingering each other's modified
bellybuttons
softly swaying their hips
while lightly brushing against
each other's hemp and cotton
hybridized jeans / yoga pants
all of it happening in a freeform haze
while attuning their attentions
to the portable technology *at hand*

Must be getting closer to
the heart of Buddhist Amerika (!)
mused the Mockman

No shit, Sherlock, mumbled Bram,
but we're still in New Mexico
or at least what they used to call
New Mexico before the Christian fundamentalists
from Colorado Springs facilitated the exodus
and expanded their base all points south
and now – from what I hear - want to call this strip of I-25
The Christ Corridor

One angel who passed by their
Cumulative Male Aura
Emitting Its Total Lack of
Originality

stuck out her tongue
long and thick and luscious
the tip of which reminded me
of a heavenly discourse I once had
with a warm steel stud on the tender
edge of my beckoning flag of freedom

But that was *me*,
when I was more patriotic
and less pathetic
so let's get back
to the shaggy dog story

On her tantalizing tongue
was a tattoo of a radiating vein
pulsating nuclear messages in
a fluorescent text scroll
transmitting weird crypto-lingo like

macramé my hairy armpits
and I'll give you secret access
to my vegan Mound's Bar

and then, parenthetically

(it'll make you crazy for cococunt!)

I got a tattoo of a soysauge wiener
on my left testicle
claimed one pirate who
coming up to the trio
identified himself as Pierce

He was clearly agitated
but like the other dudes
softly shuttling through the maze

of passive-aggressive energy
filling the space with ultimate
sanguine affection
it was a gentle pirate agitation
one that suggested he was both
calm and collected
as well as an overly stressed out
knot of terrorist insurgency
ready to powder the world
with his anthrax poetry

My nipple is pierced, said Pierce,
a little drunk or no, more than a
little drunk, how about a lot drunk
and not sure who he was talking to
or, yes, certain he was talking to
himself, out loud, so that whoever
was in his proximity would hear what
he had to say to himself, and it was
a sad loser story like so many other
sad loser stories except this time
it happened to be the sad loser story
of a trust-fund baby whose trust had become suspect
and whose year end funds were running out

Look, he said, unbuttoning his
70s silk disco shirt with floral patterning,
like I said, my nipple is pierced with
my former nose-ring
which I swore I would keep
after I tore it from
my ex-girlfriend's labia
when she said she was replacing it
with a small stainless steel stud
snuggled up inside her poontalicious
raindrop bell
so that when she started riding
her Harley up and down
the steep cobblestone streets
of our famous Beatnik City
she would gyrate herself
into nonstop orgasms

endless motorcycles
of mobile repetition
that ripped her desire to shreds

She was worse than a stoner
growing up on a Mary J. Wanna farm
totally addicted to the soft drug
of continuous orgasm

Damn, he said, talking to the
spinning disco ball above their heads,
she wanted to bring that Harley dude
to bed with us

but of course
he just wouldn't fit,
he was worse than a horse,
at least a horse has a heart
and I could FUCK HIM UP,
but this was just a balls to the wall
motherfucking motorbike

so she would go out
and ride him at three in the morning
the cool foggy breeze of the
Pacific moisture wetting up
her inner sleeves
as she drifted into
the pure bodily ambience
of her nocturnal emissions
drenched in the fluid ambiguity
of her sexuality on fire
while always trying to use
her seductive knowledge
to put the fire out

But it did no good,
he lamented,
she could never put it out

So God did it for her,
breast cancer,
and now all I got is this

nipple pierce and a limp dick
that refuses to maneuver

and as he said this
he clumsily slammed his glass down
on the bar
breaking it
and the Barkeep
had no choice but to reprimand him
peace-style

Chill, Pierce, said the Barkeep,
and try one of these,
and he poured him a shot of
Cock and Spaniel

Peace, Brother,
said Pierce,
as he slammed down the herbal narcotic
immediately forgetting who he was for about 30 seconds
before floating away one inch above the
orange shaggy wag carpet

Meanwhile three earth angels
going by the names
Rainbeau, Sprout, and Creatia
came up to the nomadic spam wanderers
and asked if they were just passing through town

which they said they were

upon which the angels inquired
as to whether there was enough room
inside the Giant Soybean Machine
for them to hitch a ride up to
Pay-Own-Ya

What's in Pay-Own-Ya? asked Mocky

Oh, doncha know? It's the new
Burning Man
except it ain't called Burning Man
anymore

What's it called? asked Bram
whose overall presence had shrunken
due to the heavy weed and
his own internal oblivion
brought on by the disappearance
of his wondergirl

It's called Gaia in the Raw
said Rainbeau

A place to dream the Eternal Now -
at least for the long weekend
she said, trying her best to
sound totally self-confident

You can write out your
endless prognosis
said Sprout
pointing to Mocky's
portable RIMMjob

There'll be 100% natural
botanicals available
gorgeous concoctions
that are made to turn you into
a world-class loverman!

No more lonerman!
responded Creatia
as if she and Sprout were
now tag-teaming the final
spam pitch

Imagine loco water & grilled wheatmeat
poured over a steaming pile of kinky quinoa
continued Creatia
in apparent vegie porno spam nonsequitur

and, Rainbeau chirped in,
not only that, but it's nice
to be able to pose before
those ubiquitous web cams

Yeah, concluded Sprout,
What You See Is What You Get

Gnomic love handles, said Rainbeau

Gelatinous wiggle room -
to flip-flop your decision-making apparatus in!
promised Creatia

Oiled palm readings
that will trace your lifeline
all the way back to the brink of
psychojizz detonation!

You'll get totally shafted, all three
chorused together

The boys eyeballed each other
not because they were confused
but because they *thought* they understood

Think potlatch
said Creatia

Think gift economy
said Sprout

And all the vegan mounds bars you can eat
chimed in Rainbeau

Gaia in the Raw
murmured Ali

Well, there's plenty of room
said Bram
and we'll be ready to roll
as soon as we chug these
Liquid Herbals

Looks like they're already
having their intended effect
mused Creatia

as she glanced down at their
collective corduroy convention
all three of the wicked stiff members
delegating their authority
while battling the bulge

You could kill an army
with those things
suggested Sprout

Or just gently inoculate
a potential ally
purred the Creatia-kitten

Either way you look at it
summarized Rainbeau
your organ donation program
has blockbuster potential!

To *Gaia in the Raw*
toasted Ali as he lifted his
tall glass of herbalized Vitamin V

Mocky and Bram lifted their glasses
and the three of them chugged
what was left

And then they all left
all six of them

Bram Mocky Sheesh Ali
Rainbeau Sprout & Creatia

They went outside
and threw their bodies into
the bed of organic greens
that was the 100% natural parking lot
where the greasy soyburger was
resting in peace
longing for a low-carb honeybun
but also
very accepting of the fact

that its whole reason for existing was to cash in
on one of those trendy no-carburetor diets
of veggie fuel & the body electric
just the pure beano
and they all hopped aboard
nestling into the brown rice
lentil upholstery
opening their wi-fi hearts
and synaptic blue tooth signals
to the Next Big Thing
on the mountain-jammed horizon

which
according to the promiscuous angels
now occupying half the space
in the moveable feast
all aboard The Mighty Beanburger
was a place called
Pay-Own-Ya

/   /   /   /

In Pay-Own-Ya
they speak a hybridized
westernspeak called
Desperanto

It's one part desperado
and one part esperanto

with a dash of sampled spam
thrown in for good measure

Think of it as a kind of
open source content schpiel -
an outlaw language / cyberpidgin
said Rainbeau,
one that grows out of
the nebulous activities
of a swollen set of
disenfranchised marketers
and former dot.com luminaries
who now - shit out of luck

and totally defaulted
(on student loans, to begin with) -
have formed a loose tribe
of wanderlusting utopians
who breastpoundingly identify themselves as
The Artificial Intelligentsia

Of which we all are a part of
whether we wish to acknowledge it
or not, chimed in Creatia,
herself squeezed tightly between
the lubricated VJ Mocky and
the patchouli-scented Sprout

Is it easy to sprachen der
Desperanto? asked Ali

Sure, confirmed Rainbeau,
you're speaking it now

Really? queried Bram
how can that be?

Look, said Creatia,
Just be yourself and let
the universal language flow
out of your embedded A.I.
like a tigress let loose
in an open field composition
of desire and rambunctious
pornosophy

Pornosophy? mused Mocky

Yep, confirmed Rainbeau,
that would be one part porno
and one part philosophy

It's like mixing the Oooh
with the Oy, said Ali,
although he had no idea
where his thought came from.

Death with desire, said Sprout

The desire to annul desire,
quipped Creatia –
to feel desire expire!

So that you don't know if
you're coming or going
said Rainbeau

Which is a place I wanna be,
spouted Sprout

As opposed to a place I've already been,
said Creatia

Such as? asked Ali

For example, Southern California,
noted Creatia, that space of mind where
the derivation is more like
like totally like totally
like   like   like

Omigod

Like, it was like,
Omigod

Like, like, you know
what I mean?

It was like, like
Omigod

It was like, like
O O O O O O O O O

I get it, said Mocky,
enough -

You don't need to be grumpy,
redoubled Sprout, just play

out the possibilities as they
dance off your tongue

Your numb tongue –

Your numb dumb
and full of cum
tongue

Just rumb-a-dumb-tongue
all over your numbskull body

Your numbskull body is just aching
for a tongue lashing

(and she leaned over and licked his sideburn)

For example, said Creatia,
take your tiger nut milk dream
and imagine the letter M

Use that as your entry level
ghost note and start receiving
transmissions from the collective
A.I.

Now (she went on)
repeat after me
(which they did)

eye

(eye)

eigh

(eigh)

oy

(oy)

we

(we)

Good, let's keep going:

oh-ooo

(oh-ooo)

ew

(ew)

ow

(ow)

Excellent! yelled Creatia

Now take that tiger nut milk dream
leaking out of the letter M -
take it in the palm of your mouth
and slowly *shape the form*

as in

May I?
My eye?

Meigh myself an eye?

Ay, are you with me, Matey?

Kinda, said Mocky

Or, said Sprout,
what about the unconditional
M-we, pronounced *mwee*
which is the polar opposite of *moi*
as in mwe mwould if mwe could
but mwe speak in foreign tongues

and are still relentlessly
caught up in the rational I

Which is the antithesis
to the artificial I
compounded Rainbeau

Mwy I can't say, but that's
the situation mwe find ourselves in

Imagine a world of Mwe
said Creatia

Mwe mwould be better off for it

Mew and I
in perpetual oy
lost in a cacophony of
ooze and oz
shaping the form
of
Mwe
on the edge of forever
milking the dream
in endless spill
of liquefied moi.

You know the drill,
said Rainbeau,
repeat after me
(which they did)

eye

(eye)

eigh

(eigh)

oy

(oy)

we

(we)

Good, let's keep going:

oh-ooo

(oh-ooo)

ew

(ew)

ow

(ow)

And that's just the start,
said Sprout – it's easy peasy -
if you can hack it

Which you can, instructed Creatia –
you can *always* hack it
that's what the open source lingospace
is all about

Hacking reality, seconded Rainbeau

At which point the three
earth angels jointly
improvised a song made out of
the tiger nut milk dream of Desperanto:

Mi linguio es know problado
Es creato ee creole ee verdado
En tellijanse o memeo danse
El macromense il microsense!

Mi linguio es know problado
Es creato ee creole ee verdado
En tellijanse o memeo danse

El macromense il microsince!

That's beautiful,
replied Mocky,
but what does it all mean?

Don't mean shit, said
Sprout, with a giggle
and slight wiggle of her
abundant cleave

Oh Sprout, teased Rainbeau,
you know that's not true

It's not that there's no meaning
it's that you need to unlearn
what you know and create alternative
patterns of recognition out of the memeo dance!

En creato, muchando illuminos, said Ali

No problado! seconded Bram

But Mocky was still disturbed.

He was slow at learning new languages,
and it made him feel "ill-timed"
in the microsense of that term.

So he decided to change the subject.

Spreading himself out
across the back of the burning burger
and looking as though he had become
transfixed and taken over by the spirit
of a renegade poet already long since corrupted
by a host of self-composed juicy viruses
he took on the persona of a tempered
Oral Reality:

Are you tired of getting infec.ted
when you try to down/load soft-ware online?

You've heard about these pills on TV,
in the news, and online, and have probably
asked yourself, "Do they really work?"
The answer is YES!

Everything anything is possible w/
Big Wood

Compulsory Catatonia! (TM)
are the makers of Big Wood,
the new, anti-insurgent medication
that is Iraq-hard and
Cro-Mag stiff!

Carry your Big Wood
like you never thought
you could!

You can take Big Wood
and disembowel a continent!

You can take Big Wood
and open up an unforgiving
chickenhawk blockage!

With Big Wood, you can achieve
terrific results and deliver
self-contradictory rationale with
neoconservative acumen!

Use this powerful
erection enhancing product
that will create stiff willies
so strong and full of themselves
that over time your lordly apparatus
will conquer entire nations!

No more preemptive ejax!

65
67
69
71
73
75
77
79
81
83
85
87
89
91
93
95
97
99
101
103
105
107
109
111
113
115

With Big Wood you only come
when YOU want to
and one thing we can guarantee you:
post-War staying power
that will defy the terrorists
of their orgasm-killing agenda!

Take Big Wood today and watch the peons
fall all over themselves treating you
as a sexual liberator!

No more torture chamber snuff films
without the money shot!

No more sentient meltdown causing
charred remains of grim disorder!

Just nonstop hooded love triangles!

Pansexual pyramids of bodily lust!

Long lost lovers on a leash!

It's better than raw cheekbone reconstruction!

Big Wood is a frolicking propaganda machine
with strategically inseminated heft!

The total complete makeover of your mind!

The total complete takeover of your mind!

It's time to unwind!

wuxhwd gln qjqxxvojipov

say goodbye

At which point Mocky closed
his eyes and fainted, or

just fell asleep from all
of the mental agitation.

He soon awoke, though, as
Bram took a fast corner and
rumbled down a dirt road a bit
so he could find a quiet spot
to take a long, warm piss.

When Bram got back to the car,
everyone (including the re-aroused
Mocky) was already out of the beanburger
standing up and staring at the surroundings.
Without even realizing it, Bram had brought them
out to a secluded dune location that
was as desolate and beautiful as
any other planet imaginable.

The still Earth, he said,
above the quiet.

It was as if they were
all in prayer.

Soon,
spontaneously,
they all reached out and took hold
of each other's hands and improvisationally
formed a circle near the crackling
soybean machine.

Still, said Bram,
the Earth.

He went on, repeating himself,
with some minor variation:

>   *The still Earth, instills*
>   *a newbirth. An illogic of*
>   *sense, details the circumstance.*
>
>   *Still, the Earth. Not still*
>   *life, nor planetary self*

portraiture, but stillness
in motion: timelessness.

The sand refuses to reflect
the narcissistic becoming of
the absent figures who walk about
its glassy shores.

Drowning in its emptiness,
the poet glosses over its
burgeoning nothingness lost
in the caress of millennia.

Only the killer beams
of the highfalutin sun
will outray this stun gun.

And with this, he absentmindedly
remembered to put his cock
back into his drawers and scoped
the scene.

We have a play, said Sprout.

A play? asked Bram.

Yes, said Rainbeau, a kind
of play, or maybe you could
call it a landscape.

A landscape? asked Ali.

Yes, said Creatia, a kind
of scenery where everyone says
what everyone says and what
everyone says is sometimes
taken lightly.

But not lightly as in not-seriously,
said Sprout, rather, this play will
play with the landscape and
the unbearable light of seeing -

that is, playing the landscape
as a kind of scenery for the play
to play itself out in.

What do you call the play?
asked Mocky.

We call it *iMuse*, confessed
Rainbeau as she adjusted all of
her iGear that was still somehow
attached to her hairy armpitted
au so naturelle body.

We shall improvise, she continued,
and the three earth angels
ran out about twenty yards skating
on the smooth glass surface of the
sun baked sand, barefooted and fancy
free, spirited body language and
matted dreadlock snakes electrifyingly
tussled about the tops of their phrenetic
    Medusa   Heads.

The silence was not so much deafening
as roaring with anticipation,
the eager beaver momentum building
like a sexual bombast ready to discharge
its megalomaniacal brilliance
onto the shredded affair they had all
quite simply bought into.

iMUSE

[every time one of the actors speaks, she contorts her body
into a different position, occasionally clawing or petting or
lightly touching one of the other actors]

> Rainbeau: Here is here. In my long short still life, I
> feel it, I feel it coming and it is great to feel it coming,
> it is great to feel it coming here in my long short still
> life.

Sprout: But I wonder, as I wander, in my great short still life, I wonder about my great short still life and its feeling for longing, its long longing and long feeling, its long feeling of wanting, and I still cannot help but wonder, what it is that makes me wander thus.

Creatia: Do you know where I come when I go? When I feel myself coming on the go? On the go, I am always coming, I am always feeling my way toward coming and while feeling my way toward coming I am going. I am feeling my way toward coming when I am going, when I am en route to coming or not necessarily feeling my way toward coming but actually coming. A long feeling is actually coming and actually going, although sometimes the long feeling feels like it is actually coming shortly.

Rainbeau: Yes, I will be coming shortly.

Sprout: But first I must come. It shouldn't take long.

Creatia: My life, that is. It shouldn't take long. Or, if it takes long, then it shouldn't be a long still feeling, a long still feeling of wonder. It should be a moving visual feeling of wander. A moving visual feeling of wander and always coming. My feeling is that we should come along shortly and when we come along we should come along wanting, and with wanting we should bring wander, and with wander we should bring feeling and only if we are loving. I am wanting to come long with feeling but only in loving.

Rainbeau: I can come without loving. I can come without loving but I cannot come without feeling. Without feeling I come shortly. Still, I cannot help but wonder what a wandering loving would feel like when longingly coming. Would it feel like going? Would it feel long?

Sprout: I can only go when I feel like coming. Without that feeling of wanting to come, I cannot go, I cannot come shortly or longingly or lovingly without that feeling. It's the coming that makes the going possible, and when the going is good, the coming is even better. It's the coming making the going that makes me feel good. I begin to feel good to go, and then the wanting comes, the wanting of the coming, comes, and I feel it, oh how I begin to feel it come.

Creatia: I begin to feel its greatness, its coming greatness, and the coming greatness comes to me like loving, and when that greatness is coming on to me like loving, I feel like I can live forever.

Rainbeau: Like I can live the long forever.

Sprout: The long coming.

Creatia: The long coming lovingly coming, forever.

All three: Goingly coming.

There was muted silence
and drippy wet crotches.

I guess that means it's time to go,
suggested Ali.

We came, we played, we went,
said Mocky.

What a scene, said Ali.

What a landscape, mused Mocky.

more girth=happy women ice abundant
more girth=happy women score led
more girth=happy women convenient
more girth=happy women voracious
more girth=happy women leaking phenotype

Meanwhile, Bram was totally preoccupied in some distant thought. He had completely forgotten about his mission to go and rescue Katt from herself, to rip her from the claws of whatever animal vortex she was presently caught in.

Was this a serious weakness on his part?

Or was he just like every other Tongue Dick and Hairy, taking advantage of whatever cool and cosmological moment the Whacked Out Gods of Potential Fornication had once again delivered to him?

Was he really such a bad bastard after all and even if he was, why the sudden guilt complex? Was he hardwired to always feel guilty whenever he got off track, whenever he noticeably digressed from the supposed road he was on? Fuck that! Especially given the fact that he would soon earmark a final denouement with no anti-climactic performance and thus clock out of the play for good?

Talk about pre-programmed Modern Living!

He would have *none* of it.

Or at least that's what one part of him was totally convinced of.

Another part of him wanted to play the good guy, the morally attuned hero (but on whose moral standard?) who would soon find Katt, to set her straight, to secure her future for her, even though deep down inside, he knew she was perfectly capable of securing her own future, despite all of her own personal insecurities.

And what of HIS personal insecurities? No question about it: he had good and plenty insecurities but why bring them up now, here, in the midst of this rambling wreck of a jalopy he was now using as a vehicle to explore his more poetic self?

And speaking of which, what happened to the so-called
poetry?

> *here it is*
> *underground teen pussy*
> *she wont quit - chasm glutinous*
> *counterintuitive glandular trajectory*
> *your daughter playing with her asshole*
> *autocannibalism facilitates the coma*

Where was I, asked Bram.

You were about to suggest that
we jump back into the carsophagus
and keep fueling ourselves to the
hactivist borderzones of Pay-Own-Ya
(someone said).

Oh yeah, right.

Let us go, he said. Let us
go, goingly and lovingly.

> *Artist! Be a tongue minesweeper*
> *orifice bodyguard constrict euphoria*
> *Fuck girls in the woods*
> *hardest task in life....*
> *Re: when it's all over*
> *Now you can have her moat bounty*

Upon entering the gates of Pay-Own-Ya
a 100+ green acre farmland on the
Western Slope of Colorado
just north of Gunnison and Black Canyon

where organic tomatoes and cherries and apples
and apricots and pears and even
the world's sweetest peaches grow
there was a tall totemic sign that declared

Spam Free Zone

and to the side of the sign was a tall black wall
about eight feet high and thirty feet wide
constructed by The Raw People
those who were the organizers
managers & participants of the
Gaia in the Raw event that was
just about to start on these very same
organic farmland premises

Next to the tall black wall –
which everyone called The Monolith -
were cans of green florescent spray paint
cans of dark yellow and red house paint
various brushes and magic markers
& colored paper & florescent tape
anything everything that could be used
to convey an individual's spam cleansing
was available at the entrance
and as part of the entry fee
($50 per car)
each person had to contribute
a spam email subject heading

one that they would forever purge from memory

The Monolith was already having
a kind of emetic effect
on the peace babies
as they scribbled their
technicolored day-glo mixed media markings
across the surface

a multilinear skidmark
of collective consciousness
at once cartoonish and eerily

reminiscent of a walk through
the virtual catacombs of deleted emails
full of the pixelated remnants
of REAL DEAD marketers
leaking a corrupt natural language

that was

as the first line high atop The Monolith stated

a shadowy something far away

which was then followed by the rest
of the language wall dripping
its unraveled hive mind
revealing the Total Mental Breakdown
of an entire People modulated by fear
and the closet dream of demarcating
a break away from the incorrigible infiltration
of phony crony capitalism and its itinerant
cache of synthetic meat poetics and randomized
terror alerts pirouetting on TV screens
projecting the stranglehold of a monstrous
sinewy synecdoche -

a shadowy something far away
protect yourself from THEM
stay secure – don't go out
tell me about it gassy amphioxis
more girth=happy women score laid
all i wanted was your bearish dacca
Let me spread my WWWormal transgressions
Big fuckpoles want to clean your ass out, good
Every man wishes he had a larger penis
stay secure – don't count on it
all i want is.. neuritis basidiomycete
easy answer: feed the birds
do you still feel the power?!

healthier, happier, harder! guinea dys
This is the best proverbial seduction - poetry
Increase. ;_ D^IC;K LENGT-H   typwisw
But why? . .
behind 3 because 3 at once will fill her up
tertiary life vision
stay secure – don't risk life, not this one!
olivetti bivalve tint convenient crocus
Dont Dare To Fcuk Bcos Ur PeNlS Is Too
Compulsory Catatonia – are we there yet?
Never been easier
jujube sancho synonym decade
Get those inches scherzo cheney
My secretary, who had been taught to
more pleasure for you and her trounce
soft at incredibly low prices
Bx we value you.
more girth=happy women lice abundant
look here to find out kosher spleenworm
your daughter fingering her asshole
orifice bodyguard constrict euphoria
counterintuitive glandular trajectory
beatnik teen pussy needs hipster!
Artist mindsweeper
Our little secret
Compulsury Catatonia – get the consumer edge!
hardest task in life....
dont ignore your problems!
stay secure – increase your credit line
phenotype
drunk mosquitoes rid de-pollute you
Now you can have her moat bounty
i told you so civic pandemonium
Fuck dead animals in the woods
sacrifice a little - complicitly marry
Re: your aftermath is one big death tax credit!
just as i thought; hatred was an accessory
hear it is – your conch shell memory
Are you a player? gift economy
The solid Power of Understanding fails
eliminate unpleasant body odors
anus walnut cracking - dig in!
Stop feeling bad about yourself!!

100
102
104
106
108
110
112
114
116
118
120
122
124
126
128
130
132
134

sinewy synecdoche -
the words spun in Bram's mind
as he was finally coming to
again
after all of the distractions
although who is to say what is a distraction
and what is a harmonious digression
within a digression within
a digression
and how these stories tell a greater story
of how stories get told
or better
how they are lived
alive
in the present
an organism filtering endless threads
endless stories that connect and disconnect
yet somehow keep a momentum going
the warm embodiment of a serial juggernaut
knotted in contradictions
and contradistinctions
the yesno insideout upsidedown manwoman
on the edge of forever
simultaneously and continuously digressing and delaying
differing and deferring
ones ultimate persuasion
from meeting its final destination
its once and for all closure to end all closures
the cloture of bane existence
boning up for the final showdown
at the A-OK corral
lassoing you in for one last promise
one last postmortem heavenly product
heavily discounted!

As these morbid thoughts rolled through his brain
like a train of moods pulsating along
his emotionally scarred memory tracks
he realized that he could not just let her go
that he was going to forever find himself

in love with her no matter what she did
and who she did it with
that this was one of those All Strings Attached
performances of psychotic puppetry
and that her own special brand of
in-your-face infopornography
was just a cover for having to prove
something
anything
to herself

or so he thought

but what did he know?

Maybe the woman he loved was
a true believer in exhibitionism
and felt that by sharing their sex life
with whoever was willing to pay
$15 a month to tune in to their website
she was somehow sharing a political
belief system that had something to do with
free love free verse free thinking
but even so, you had to pay for it,
always.

The Bramster thought of
booting up his RIMMjob
so that he could access the Superfuckalicious website
which he imagined might reveal something new
something that would point him in the right direction
not to rescue Katt per se
but to rescue himself now
and in the process
to further motivate his time-worn body
through the psychogeographical spaces
of his body-brain-apparatus achievements
so as to eventually become emptied of experience
emptied of energy
emptied of everlasting –

what?

It was hopeless -

He knew it was hopeless -

Here he was at the language wall
The Monolith
entering Pay-Own-Ya's own
Gaia in the Raw
with a traveling tribe
of neo new age digital iBods
who were going to have the time
of their lives -

And what would he do?

Would he too have the time of his life?

Would he continue to

   play the game?

Or was that feeling of already being
played going to stick in him like
an intelligent claw taking hold of
his interiorized landscape ripping
it to shreds, so that his sorry sack
of skin would reveal itself to be nothing
but an exfoliated scumbag of emotions
torn to nothingness where even the dust
and final drops of his slow dripping blood
were now being gradually molded into a crusty
scab of dirty blobmatter that would quickly erode
in the sands of telegenic realtime   ?

That wasn't even a sentence.

But it felt like one
and that's all that mattered to him now.

Sheesh Ali handed him a red spray paint can.

Purge thyself, was all he said and Bram
approached The Monolith
writing the first spam-thing on his mind:

junky trickster's almighty serum?

At which point the earth angels
all three of them, started shooting
water pistols loaded with LSD-infused
rosewater, the playful spritzing bubbling
all over his face and neck and hands
and eventually seeping into his thirsty mouth
while the trio chanted some unintelligible mantra
that would supposedly rid him of the
preoccupational demons that had been
corrupting his smooth lathered dreams
while using their hands to massage his neck
six hands moving in sync and slowly
taking hold of his Thick Tenseness
the hands turning into mouths
open holes full of wet hardened
tongues digging deep into his curved musculature
a trio of circulating blissballs deep tonguing
his extremities as if gorging on
nothing but raw potential.

His conscious thoughts warped

body stretched and prone

to sensual detox

eyes closed torso lifting
lightness
elevation

organs without body

de strat I fied

i.d.

at the door

blown

WIDE

OPEN

When he awoke he found himself dreaming

Or if not dreaming then visualizing

transported into another state of hyperimprovisational

composing

Either it was happening or it wasn't happening

Or if it was happening then it was happening with him or without him

Or if it was happening with him

It was happening with him as an insideout upsidedown yesno manwoman

It was happening under a huge tarp covering a huge stage and when he opened his eyes he saw or did not see but hallucinated or dreamed he saw onstage a green painted body that dripped radioactive yellow paint from various hanging genitalia and that kept swatting flies and mosquitoes with its long eel-like nose that could have been part snake and part elephant trunk or just new-age reptilian schnoz although no one knew for sure what kind of creature this thing was freaking to be, but finally it identified itself as The Crankworm and without any ado began to recite what it referred to as its nuclear poetry:

Who is the chimp who champs at the bit?

And why does he need to feel the edge
of all of our world's existence for us?

The chimp is selected as a leader and
with this selection mouths improprieties
without pity, without piety.

For example, he'll say:

"For sustained, controlled fusion reactions,
a fission bomb obviously cannot be used
to trigger the reaction."

But when questioned further, he has
no reaction. His teleprompter has
no answers and neither does he.

Riding his hotheaded hobby horse into
the blue screen mission accomplished sunset,
the cowboy chimp senses that the enthusiasm
for his heavenly endorsed legacy
is slipping away.

Should he start a nuclear war on his way out?

He wonders if that might not backfire.

The real question is, what would properly
Jesu-fy him to the polling masses?

"The difficulties of controlled fusion,"
he stammers, "center on the containment
of the nuke-ler fuel at the extremely
high temperatures necessary for fusion."

But he knows nothing about fusion,
only that he disdains fusion cooking.

He is a meat and potatoes boy.

With all of this desire for fusion,
comes more confusion, and as Confucius
might say:

"Everyone drinks and eats, but few know
the real taste of what has been drunk or eaten."

The cowboy chimp knows only the taste of burgers,
but thinks he deserves the taste of victory.

Still, after all baboon buffoonery, he comes
on like a simultaneous and continuous Fusion Man
whose keyboards corrupt.

His ill-tempered euphoria
over the equipotentiality of all
suddenly imagined mushroom clouds,
clouds his mind.

Clueless, he talks about Jesus and God
as if the disease eating away inside his skull
were part of the autocannibalism process and
all one had to do was cook up another batch
of unbelievable tripe and the hungry masses
would slurp it up in a 9-11 second.

But this is to lose sight of the extra
terrestrials whose artificial life
his policies are effectively nuking
out of existence.

The masses have become de-massified,
and knowingly imbibe drops of acidophilus
so that the flora in their gut and the fauna
prancing about in their brains can sustain
another feeding regimen.

But can they really survive or are they
destined to a life of wannabe indebtedness?

His nuclear war has no value in their biosphere,
and the starving robots know it. Deep down –
deep in the sludge vortex of their polluted bodies,
they know the grease monkey is trying to lubricate
their tamest of dreams.

So it's time to say goodbye.
Goodbye King Nuke-Lear,
goodbye hamburger boy.

Next time you are hungry and need a Daddy-Ego Fix,
throw your meatbrain into the microwave and nuke it.

And with that, the Crankwork took a deep yoga bow,
curling into a foetus position until finally vanishing
in the dusk turning into darkest of night.

The huge crowd spread across the farm field roared.

Nuke it. That was enough, thought Bram
as he felt himself being mounted.

A dry drunk always has the option of nuking it.

It's more convenient that way.

Once nuked, always nuked –
    if only to enucleate ones lack of vision from the core of history.

Have you ever tried to take a piece of meat,
a tender loin with tendons streaking through
its marbled hallway of glassy fat and layered protein
and just nuke the hell out of it?

And then nuke it again

    and again?

and still yet again?

Bram had. What it becomes is

postanimal.

Bram could relate.

He thought of something Emerson once wrote:
"Our love of the real
draws us to permanence,
but health of body consists
in circulation, and sanity
of mind in variety or facility
of association. We need change
of objects."

Down below him in front of the stage
and behind the big gorgeous thing that
has now successfully strapped itself on to him
he thinks he sees the earth angels,
Rainbeau, Sprout & Creatia,
joined by at least 20 others just like them,
create a Sacred Earth Circle, a diabolical force
fielding all of the available energy circulating
underneath the now rising full moon
where he feels the pull of his blood setting him
into the traps of yet another voluptuous cycle.

The angels are chanting their Songs of Oblivion
and in so doing are successfully sucking into
their Collective Psychosphere the lost souls
of Sheesh Ali and VJ Mocky, one after the other
quickly disappearing into the symbiotic vortex:
first Ali the forever in shape athlete and cultural warrior,
and next Mocky the hyperimprovisational visual poet-performer,
the two whose combined presence makes me the man I am today,
or so thought Bram as he himself, easily seduced
by the scene, allowed his roaming lightform of purely
alienated bodily lust to slowly slide into the pleasure
of endless gyrations slowly taking over his stiffened Life,

his eyes closed and almost sleeping and knowing
it was a smooth surrender into something warm and familiar.

He took what he had, what he had been given,
at birth, and he watched it grow. And as it grew
he realized he was no longer the man he used to be,
that, in fact, he was on the verge of changing, again.

Lost in the thick creamy texture of his deep and long coming.

His eyes closed tight imagining the earth angels
as they slowly enter his skin and begin the begin, tooling
around inside his insides, a kind of synchronized
swimming for 23 mermaids of underworld lust,
scaling his interior walls climbing and clawing
their way into his vision so that he could no longer
keep his eyes open, their collective thrust pulling his
lids shut.

His dreamy eyes seeing nothing but feeling,
nothing but a raw feeling completely taking over
his body, riding his torso from above as if
this horse's dick of a man were for her pure bodily pleasure,
a ramrock hard and pulsating dildo of total convenience,
and the experience of it being him, the Adamic other
with curls on his head and light green eyes finally shut
and letting her have her way with him.

Her towering young body deranging
his senses more than any runt poet
could ever dream of, the clarity of his vision
behind closed eyes seeing nothing, nothing
but raw feeling, and in this raw feeling, feeling
more than her, feeling Her Body, feeling it
smother him in front of the cameras.

There they were. Again.
Back in front of the cameras.

   Underneath the rising full moon
on a makeshift stage with a makeshift bed
while a makeshift ska band was playing its driving rhythms

out in the middle of nowhere, the erehwon vortex,
thousands of people now watching them
from the depths of the crowd, as well as
tens of thousands more from various
net connected RIMMjobs all over the planet.

There they were, live. Again.
Under the soft, slow drip of a heavenly rain,
in front of the cameras.

Soon the soft, slow drip turned into a sprinkle
and the sprinkle gave way to the steady rhythm
of a light yet persistent rain and then it gradually became
a stronger more forceful even more persistent rain
while the ska band kept pounding its driving beats
and then there were jolting cracks of thunderous lightning
that hit at the core of the crowd's collective heart and
they all felt themselves giving into Nature, letting it pour
it's wet electrical storm all over their by now naked
bodies and as if on cue, everyone was rolling in the thick
puddles of aromatic mud like pigs playing in shit,
a pack of cyberhillbillies fucking each other like
mad dogs in heat, and Bram opened his eyes, finally,
just for a moment.

He too was in heat.

And in that quick glimpse of the world mauling
him from above, he felt bigger than he had ever
felt before, bigger than what he had been born with,
a bigness so huge that it positioned him well beyond
the syntax of ego-driven psychobabble and its scholarly discontents.

He soon closed his eyes again and could, for the first time,
smell what could only be Her Body on him. The rain was coming
all over them, washing away nothing, only layering more dirt
and chemical by-products from up high in the corporate sky,
and this made him want her more, so he let her know this
by grabbing her perfect ass in both of his hands and moaning
a loud gut-wrenching grunt that made it clear he was close
to coming inside her.

The cameras were still rolling but nobody was watching, least of all him with his eyes permanently shut tight.

Kendall, he whispered above the clash of the tinny rain –

Bram – she replied, stopping short of going somewhere –

Here it comes – he could barely speak

I'm coming – she said

Here it comes – his voice was a crack of glitch

I'm coming – she said – *I'm really coming!*

Me too!

Ahhhg!

Tired Of Losing Trades?
Cum-too Wives!
88% of women are unsatisfied
feel the vitality! Algebraic
Seeking the Man or Woman of your dreams?
Re: when it's all over

LaVergne, TN USA
17 August 2009
155050LV00012B/121/A

9 780978 549978